The Travellerde to

LOVE

HELEN NICHOLL

·THE·
BLACK
·STAFF·
PRESS

All characters appearing in this work are fictitious.
Any resemblance to real persons,
living or dead, is purely coincidental.

First published in 2015 by Blackstaff Press
4D Weavers Court
Linfield Road
Belfast BT12 5GH

Typeset by KT Designs, St Helens, England

Printed in Berwick-upon-Tweed by Martins the Printers

A CIP catalogue for this book is available from the British Library

ISBN 978 0 85640 940 0

www.blackstaffpress.com

Thanks to my family and friends and to the Literary Ladies for their unfailing encouragement and support, but most of all to Kelly McCaughrain, to Cary Meehan, whose *Guide to Sacred Ireland* sent me travelling in the first place, and to Patsy Horton and all her lovely team at Blackstaff.

Chapter 1

When I first came to Northern Ireland I knew almost nothing about the country, beyond the fact that it was home to Socrates O'Shea, with whom I had fallen deeply in love. I had been warned it was a damp and dangerous place most sensible travellers avoided, but by the time I realised that the greatest danger to my health and wellbeing came not from the so-called Troubles – or indeed the weather, which was unrelentingly cold and wet – but from Socrates himself, it was too late, because I'd gone and married him.

However, on that long-ago night when I first arrived in Belfast, I was barely twenty, and full of the optimism of youth. Even the wail of sirens and the noise of distant explosions seemed just part of the adventure as we sped through the city and out to what I believed to be the relative safety of the O'Sheas, where Mrs O'Shea was hiding in a bend of the stairs and muttering prayers. It wasn't the sound of bombs going off that worried her: she had seen a photograph that Socrates had taken of me in London, and owing to some quirk of developing, I had turned out rather dark. At the time there were very few foreigners living in Northern Ireland, and Mrs O'Shea had been told I came from Africa, and was alarmed.

Despite this inauspicious beginning, we quickly grew to like each other, and when, soon after our marriage, Socrates and I moved abroad, she took great pride in Socrates's rapid success. Not many people, she used to say, could boast that they had a son who was so quick to grasp a business opportunity. Unfortunately, this was true – but as so many of the people involved are still alive, and Socrates himself is, as far as I know, still wanted by the police, I shall say no more about those years. Besides, when all is said and done, he is still the father of my four children, and it was with the two youngest that I finally returned to Belfast some years later. By then I had managed to extricate myself from the marriage, my older children had left home and it seemed sensible to bring the twins back to complete their education in a place which they knew from frequent visits, and where they still had some family connections.

Belfast was a very different city from the one that I remembered. Where there had been barricades and checkpoints, there were now pavement cafes and crowds of people going about their normal business. And before long we too had settled into our new lives. Seamus and Nuala were accepted into the sixth form of a college known for its sporting achievements, after an interview in which I am afraid they gave a slightly misleading impression of their own athleticism: drifting lazily down the Zambezi has little in common, after all, with rowing up the Lagan at dawn. And I stopped expecting to hear the call of louries and hoopoes, or the sound of crickets, and resigned myself instead to the sound of traffic, and the cries of gulls in the grey skies overhead.

We rarely heard from Socrates, but when we did it was always from a new address, or country, from which I concluded that he was at least keeping one jump ahead of his creditors. I don't think any of us worried about him – if ever a man was likely to survive, it was Socrates – but I did worry about the future. So, as soon as the twins were settled at school, I began to look for a job – a search I combined with the pleasure of rediscovering the city on foot. And it was on one of these exploratory days that I stumbled upon the Good Intentions Bookshop.

I had been drifting down Botanic Avenue, past Archibald's Antiques (which was to play such an unexpected part in my life) when my eye was drawn to the window of a shop further down the road and I found myself peering into the dim cave that was Good Intentions. I saw at once that it was one of the last of its kind: a small, jumbled charity bookshop, stuffed with unlikely treasures, and staffed by what appeared, at first sight, to be amiable lunatics. This first impression was not entirely wrong: over time I came to know the shop well and the volunteers who ran it were notable, even in a city of eccentric characters, for their peculiar charm and for their decided, and frequently opposing, views. But the main reason why I have such a soft spot for the Good Intentions Bookshop is that it was there, several years later, that I first met Albert.

What can I say about Albert? He was very tall and thin and as bald as an egg. It was what I first noticed about him: a gleaming skull bobbing along between the bookshelves. Closer inspection revealed an interesting line in layers of well-worn tweed and corduroy, and very old and expensive-looking shoes. From this I deduced, quite rightly, that the object of my inspection rarely, if ever, bought anything new. From a distance he wasn't promising, but then he turned and looked me full in the face. My friend Rita – a great authority on men – once stopped me halfway through my list of some new prospect's sterling qualities: 'Yes, that's all very well,' she said, before cutting straight to the chase as always, 'but does he make your knees knock?'

Albert turned out to have as mesmerising a pair of eyes as I have ever encountered, and they could have heard my knees knocking in Ballymena.

It was with some difficulty that I dragged my gaze away from his and down to the book he had been examining.

'The Traveller's Guide to Ancient County Down,' I said. 'What a lucky find!'

'Do you know it?' He had a beautiful husky voice.

'Well no, not really, but it looks fascinating.'

'Then you must have it.' He thrust the book into my hands.

'Oh no, I couldn't possibly! You found it first, Mr …'

'Albert,' he said. 'Albert Morrow. And you are?'

'Johanna. Johanna van Heerden.'

'Ah, Johanna …'

We might well have stood there longer, foolishly transfixed, if a head I knew well hadn't popped out just then from behind a pile of books, and fixed us with a dragon-like stare.

'You've got exactly two minutes before I lock the door,' it said, 'so if you are planning on actually buying anything, you had better be quick about it.'

It was Dolores, commander-in-chief of the volunteer army, and a woman who has no truck with pandering to the customer. Albert didn't argue: he handed over a fiver and ushered me out of the shop. There was another poor hopeful trying to get in, but Dolores simply slammed the door in his face and switched out the lights.

We stood outside, shivering in the sudden cold; then Albert said, 'I don't suppose you'd like a cup of coffee, while we argue over who gets custody of the book?'

In the end it stayed with me, because, by the time we parted two hours later, we had agreed to set out on the first of our journeys together. I was to consult *The Traveller's Guide to Ancient County Down* and choose our destination. By then it was apparent to me that I was embarking on an altogether more complicated, and possibly hazardous, journey, but I didn't care: the excitement of planning the trip, and the memory of Albert's eyes, kept any doubts at bay.

I had also offered to bring a picnic. I am particular about picnics: they must contain cold chicken or sausages, or little poppy seed pies, and there must be a variety of cheese and fruit, and chocolate. Albert, whom I rightly suspected of being an apple and sandwich man, had undertaken to provide the transport, and as his car (unlike his clothes) turned out to be a lot newer and more reliable than mine, it was a happy arrangement all round.

Our goal on that first day was the Legananny Dolmen and the directions were clear: we should take the Newcastle road to Ballynahinch then turn towards Dromara and carry on south through Finnis until we reached the first of several signposts to the dolmen – and so it proved. Albert was overwhelmed.

'Well done!' he exclaimed. 'What a piece of navigation!'

'I'm only reading the map,' I said.

'Not many women can read maps,' he replied, taking his eyes off the road to gaze at me with admiration, and narrowly missing a hedge.

'Turn here,' I said. 'There should be a place to park just ahead.'

At the time, of course, I didn't realise that Albert had as little sense of direction as a bubble, but I did feel a degree of pride as we turned up the farm lane and saw, rising before us, a glorious dolmen. The author of *The Traveller's Guide to Ancient County Down*, M. Heaney, had described it as 'most poised and graceful' and M. Heaney had got it right. Two elegant pillar stones, as tall as Albert, and a shorter end stone supported a great soaring slab of granite. Against the winter sky it was dramatic.

'Oh Albert!' I said. 'My first dolmen!'

I walked around it and under it. I leaned against its ancient sides and stroked the pitted surface of its pillars. And if you think this a somewhat excessive reaction to a pile of old stones, then I can only say that we had nothing like it in Gauteng: as you might be fascinated by the sight of an elephant in the bush, so was I entranced by the alien beauty of the dolmen. It helped, of course, that the day was unusually clear, with a sweeping view of hills and valleys rolling away to the horizon, and that Albert had taken my hand.

From the Legananny Dolmen, a series of turns took us to a junction from which the road winds all the way up to Windy Gap. There we found a small car park, with picnic tables dotted about the hillside, and spectacular views in all directions.

'According to M. Heaney, that lane will lead us to a little Mass garden,' I said, pointing to a pathway on the opposite side of the road. 'Do we have time to investigate before we have our lunch?'

'I can probably hold out another ten minutes,' said Albert.

So we followed the lane uphill to a gate, and there, hidden in a dip of the hill and shielded by a circular hedge, was the tiny Mass garden. We spent some moments peering through the gate at the peaceful, secret spot with its rock altar and evidence of careful tending, then we circled back through grazing sheep, and down to our waiting picnic.

At a table above the car park, we sat in the winter sunshine and feasted on miniature pork pies, chicken and salad. We had two types of cheese, and moist, crumbling wheaten bread, and we raised our glasses of crisp white wine (a lot for me, a little for him) as we toasted the success of our first journey, and drank to the next. Then we set down our glasses and looked deep into each other's eyes …

Another good thing about Windy Gap is that there's nobody there but sheep.

By the time we returned to Belfast it was getting dark. I had moved a few miles down the coast after my two youngest children left home, and as we neared the turn-off for my house, the conversation fell away. I worried that Albert's silence was a sign of some doubt or regret but when we drew up at the gate, he leaped out of the car and insisted on helping to carry the picnic things into the hall. Then he stood on the threshold, dithering.

'I don't suppose,' he began – but a sudden overhead creaking caused him to break off mid-sentence. As he glanced upwards, his expression changed to one of alarm. 'A man with an enormous moustache is looking over your banisters!' he hissed.

'That's my landlord, Sticky Wicket,' I replied. 'He lives

upstairs. Go away, Sticky Wicket.' I had raised my voice but I was looking steadily at Albert as we listened to the sound of retreating footsteps and a door closing overhead.

I spoke more softly: 'What is it that you don't suppose, Albert?'

'Well ... that you might perhaps like to ask me in for a coffee, Johanna?'

I smiled. I reached up and grasped his tweed lapels with one hand as I pulled him towards me; with the other I slammed the door shut behind his back.

Dolores would have been proud of me.

Chapter 2

Two days later Albert and I re-emerged, blinking, into winter sunlight. We had found it impossible to part before this, but in the end, the demands of the outside world, and sheer exhaustion, drove us out. Passion, of course, is not considered proper or sensible in the middle-aged, and as my children are constantly on the lookout for signs of dementia (at which point they will whip me into a home faster than you can say 'feeble-minded'), I shall say no more, except to observe that when love strikes you down, the fire burns just as sweetly whether you are seventeen or seventy.

Now, as Albert climbed into his car and I waved him goodbye, I realised that Sticky Wicket had appeared at my elbow and was also waving.

'Sound chap,' he said. 'Met him yesterday when he was taking out your bin. Likes cricket.'

This was news to me, but I filed it away for future reference. I already knew a great deal about Albert's tastes and interests, and more importantly, his past. In Albert's case this was more complicated than most, although in those early days I was unaware of the full extent of these complications.

'I must say you're looking jolly well, Johanna.' Sticky Wicket regarded me with something close to admiration in his bulging eye, and such was my newfound feeling of peace and goodwill to all mankind that I turned and beamed.

'Thank you, Sticky Wicket,' I said. Then I went back in to my strangely empty flat.

Fortunately there was no time to brood – it was nine o'clock and I had a job to go to. Three days a week, for the last few years, I had opened the doors of Archibald's Antiques at ten in the morning and closed them again at four. On Tuesdays, Wednesdays and Thursdays I shared the tiny over-stuffed cave that was Archibald's with a cat called Morris and the occasional customer. Morris was an unrewarding animal but he tolerated my presence; the customers were the usual mixture of bargain-hunters, lost souls and, occasionally, genuine collectors of antiques. The last tended not to stay long.

The Good Intentions Bookshop is not far from Archibald's Antiques and I was in the habit of calling in there after four o'clock, to browse until it was time to catch my train. On this particular afternoon I arrived to find Dolores attempting to sell an ancient book on tropical diseases to a young man who had unwisely asked for help in finding an African travel guide.

'You cannot be too careful,' Dolores was saying. 'My niece Veronica caught E. coli from kissing a giraffe.'

'Why was she kissing a giraffe?' asked a small, anxious-looking woman who was hovering beside the counter.

'Probably because nothing human would have offered,' said a voice in my ear, and I turned to see Sybilla standing behind me.

'Hello, Sybilla,' I said. 'How's Percy?' Percy was Sybilla's parrot, an African Grey to which she was devoted. I had a parrot myself, once upon a time, so it was a mutual interest.

'Actually, Johanna, I was going to ask you if you'd look after Percy next weekend. I'm going on a walking trip with Dolores and she objects to him coming with us.'

'Too right,' said Dolores, whose customer seized this moment of inattention to flee the shop. 'Filthy things. God knows what you'd catch from them.'

'Why can't he stay at home with Roger?' I asked. Roger was Sybilla's husband and he rarely went anywhere.

'Percy doesn't like Roger.'

'Who does?' said Dolores under her breath.

'I'm so sorry, Sybilla,' I said, 'but I'm going away myself next weekend.'

And it was true. Albert and I had already had two telephone conversations since our parting that morning, and in the evening I opened the first of his emails …

✉ From: aj.morrow@googlemail.co.uk
   To: johannavanheerden@hotmail.com

   Johanna, my sweet sweet love, I can't
   believe that I have found you. It
   astonishes me how well we get along
   together. Before I go to sleep I want to
   tell you that the last two days have been
   the most wonderful of my life. Can we
   meet tomorrow for coffee?
   Albert

✉ From: johannavanheerden@hotmail.com
   To: aj.morrow@googlemail.co.uk

   My darling Albert - I can hardly believe
   that I am anyone's sweet sweet love but I
   think I must be because I have been lit
   up all day like an electric sign - I have
   been giving shocks to anyone who stands
   too close! Of course we must meet for
   coffee. Phone me in the morning. Sleep
   tight, my love,
   Johanna

On Wednesday there was another ...

✉ From: aj.morrow@googlemail.co.uk
   To: johannavanheerden@hotmail.com

   My sweet darling,
   I have been making plans for our weekend

```
   - would you like to do a tour of
Strangford Lough? But I don't think I
can wait until Friday to see you so if I
knocked on your door tomorrow evening,
would you let me in?
Albert
```

✉ From: johannavanheerden@hotmail.com
To: aj.morrow@googlemail.co.uk

```
Of course I will let you in and I would
go with you to Strangford Lough or any
other place you care to name.
I wish you were here right now.
Love, love, love,
Johanna
```

There were more emails of course, but I think that's enough to give a flavour of our early exchanges. And so, on Friday morning, in a haze of middle-aged love, Albert and I set off on our second adventure.

Strangford is a sea lough, deep and long and studded with islands – little drowned drumlins that rise above the surface of the water and are home to seals and a multitude of birds. We drove down the western side, along the road that leads to Mahee Island and Nendrum, where the remains of a Celtic monastery are protected by three concentric, stone-walled enclosures that circle the hillside; where bluebells grow on the slopes in spring; and where the view sweeps out over the lough. That morning, that I first stepped through the little gate and climbed the hill, it was winter and there were no bluebells, but the stillness and beauty of the place – and an undeniable current of something old and holy running beneath my feet – struck me dumb. I am an atheist and rarely lost for words, but on this occasion I was shaken.

From Nendrum we took the road that leads on to Ardmillan and Killinchy: a winding country route, twisting along past Skettrick Island, which is linked by a causeway to the mainland, and from the highest point of which there is a wonderful view of Strangford Lough. We stopped there briefly, before driving on to Killyleagh, a village that charmed me with its fairytale castle, and the pub where Albert and I ate beef and Guinness pie in the privacy of a tiny wooden booth.

'I suppose you've been here many times?' I said, as I wiped up the last of the gravy with a piece of crusty bread.

'A few,' he replied, 'but never in such delightful company. And you've no idea how much pleasure it gives me to rediscover it like this.'

I reached out and squeezed his hand. 'Well, you've no idea what a pleasure it is for me to be driven around by you, and to see so many places I had no idea existed. If we keep this up, I'll be able to write a guide to County Down myself!'

'Oh we'll keep it up, all right,' Albert promised, 'and when we're finished with County Down, we'll go on to all the rest.'

It was a light-hearted exchange, but it was in a little corner shop in Killyleagh later in the day that I bought the first of the notebooks I would use to keep a detailed record of our travels.

From Killyleagh we drove to Downpatrick, but winter days are short and it seemed wiser not to stop but to press on to Strangford, with a brief stop at Castle Ward.

'There is one little detour we could make, though, if we have time.' I had a map spread out on my lap, together with *The Traveller's Guide*. 'According to M. Heaney, a turning to the left will take us to Audleystown Court Cairn, which is a wedge-shaped cairn with shallow courts at either end.'

'It sounds very promising,' Albert agreed – and with that readiness to explore that I found so endearing, he launched the car down yet another of the little roads that criss-cross the countryside like cobwebs. We found the cairn without trouble and, close by, a holy well with the charming name of Toberdoney. To anyone with an interest in such things, it is worth the detour; however, if ancient burial sites do not excite you, you should continue along the Strangford Road and enter Castle Ward by the main gate.

Castle Ward is an eighteenth-century property belonging to the National Trust, and a monument to incompatible tastes, one side being designed in the classical style admired by the then Lord Bangor, the other in the Gothic, as preferred by his wife. On that occasion it was still closed for the winter months, so we stayed just long enough to admire the grounds and the views across the lough, before driving on to Strangford.

Our original plan had been to cross to Portaferry and stay there overnight. But by now the afternoon had darkened, the wind had risen, and the sea was rough. As luck would have it, the pub where we stopped had a blazing fire and a room for the night, and so we stayed in Strangford and took the ferry the next morning, over the wild grey waters to Portaferry, where we breakfasted, to the detriment of our arteries, on the full Ulster fry.

As Albert poured me a second cup of coffee, I spread the map on the table and traced our return journey up the east side of the lough.

'As I see it there are three possibilities open to us: we could take the most direct route north, or we could follow M. Heaney's directions to Cooey's Wells, where there are a couple of holy wells and a ruined church. But this would take us away from Strangford Lough and towards the sea. The third choice appears to be a little road that hugs the shoreline and joins up later with the main road north. What do you think?'

Albert regarded me with the wonderment of a man who could no more tell north from south than walk upside down. 'My darling,' he said, 'the choice is yours.' And the way he said 'my darling' turned my bones to butter.

'Then I propose that we follow the shore. After all, this is supposed to be a circuit of the lough. Cooey's Wells will keep.'

We did in fact return to Cooey's Wells at a later date, and

found that there are three: one for drinking, one for washing, and one with healing properties. As I had recently injured an ankle, I thought it worth submerging my foot, but I noticed no improvement. If anything, there was a slight increase in my discomfort. When I told Dolores of my experience, she said, 'Don't be ridiculous, Johanna – you have to be a Catholic for it to work. Protestants and atheists haven't got a prayer. *And* you're a foreigner.'

It was a wild and beautiful day when Albert and I set off along the eastern side of the lough. The tide was rushing in, clouds were racing overhead, and the colours of the land and sea changed constantly as the sun came and went through fitful showers of rain.

'We'll come back in the summer,' Albert promised, when the road finally turned inland and away from the lough. 'We'll bring a picnic, and we'll paddle.'

I laughed. 'I can't imagine it ever being warm enough for me to paddle! But I'll look forward to the picnic.' I looked down at the map and traced our route. 'Greyabbey is the next place we come to. Is there an abbey there?'

'There was,' said Albert, 'and the ruins are worth a visit, but they won't be open today. If we press on, though, we might just get a walk around Mount Stewart before the rain sets in.'

Mount Stewart is another National Trust property, famous for its gardens, and justly so: the house is interesting enough, with some notable furniture, and there is a charming Temple of the Winds overlooking Strangford Lough, but it is the grounds that are the glory of the estate.

The house is closed until early March, as are the formal gardens, but in February you can walk, as we did, through the lakeside area, or follow one of the many woodland paths that loop between the ancient trees and banks of flowering shrubs.

'I'm sorry we can't see all the gardens,' Albert said, as we completed our circuit of the lake. 'They are quite something, you know, and there are some wonderfully sinister stone monkeys that I think you'd like. But we'll come back in the spring or summer.'

'I'd like that very much,' I replied, 'although it's been a wonderful day as it is, and you are an excellent guide: you seem to know about everything.'

'My parents were pillars of the Belfast Natural History and Philosophical Society,' said Albert. 'As children we were always being dragged off on educational outings. My sisters used to complain bitterly, but in my case it was the beginning of a lifelong interest – and it's nice to be able to indulge it now that I've retired.'

I already knew that Albert's working life had been spent in the forgotten passages of the Classics department at Queen's University, that his two sisters lived abroad, and that we had a surprising number of interests in common. Now, as the rain which had threatened all day began at last to fall in earnest, and we sprinted towards the car, I thought again how happy I was, and how lucky we were to have found each other.

And I know what you are thinking: was it all so romantic, so idyllic? Reader, go and pour yourself a fortifying glass of wine – or better still, a large gin and tonic. Real life is waiting just around the corner.

Chapter 3

Albert lived at 16 Chestnut Avenue, a tall thin house in the south of the city, and next door, at number 18, lived his ex-wife, Carmel. It was at number 18 that he and Carmel had lived for most of their turbulent married life, and where they had been joined in due course by Norah and Rosie, whose childish voices had provided lighter notes in the discordant symphony of flying crockery (Carmel) and furious silences (Albert) that formed the background music to their days.

It was shortly after Rosie's fifteenth birthday that Albert had finally moved out – and into the house next door. Thus was peace restored to Chestnut Avenue, and with the girls free to move at will between the two houses, Albert had congratulated himself on having caused as little disruption to their lives as possible. It was, he said, an eminently civilised arrangement. So, when he ushered me through the gate one early spring evening, I was looking forward not just to my first night in Albert's house, but to it being the first of many such visits.

However, we were only halfway up the garden path when a window flew up in the house next door and a voice rang out.

'I see you, Albert Morrow,' it yelled. 'Adulterer!'

Albert propelled me up the path and through the door with surprising speed. It was not an auspicious start, and even before we had passed through the hallway and into a long kitchen at the back of the house, I had started to revise my expectations. The kitchen itself had a certain idiosyncratic charm, with books heaped everywhere, and on the shelves a clutter of objects that reflected Albert's many interests, but the muffled crescendo of crashes and thumps coming from next door was beginning to cause me serious concern.

'I'm so sorry, Johanna.' Albert removed a pile of books from a chair and invited me to sit down at the kitchen table before uncorking a bottle and pouring two glasses of wine; then he reached across the table for my hand. 'I thought Carmel was away – I wouldn't have brought you home if I'd known she was back: she's rather highly strung.'

There was the sound of splintering glass outside. The woman was clearly unhinged.

I sipped my wine and took a moment before I spoke. 'Does she always react like this when you bring someone home?'

'She hasn't really had much cause to – until now,' Albert replied.

There was another loud thud, then a crash.

'But why would she accuse you of adultery? You've been

divorced for … what? Five years?'

'Well,' he shifted uncomfortably, 'I've been meaning to talk to you about that. The fact is that we have been separated for five years, but not actually divorced. I realise that I may, inadvertently, have given you the impression that we were divorced – and in my own mind, I do assure you, Johanna, I most certainly am – but as far as Carmel is concerned, divorce has never been an option.'

It is perhaps because I grew up speaking two languages that I always choose my words with care, and the more upset I am, the more carefully I speak. Now I took a deep, slow breath.

'Albert,' I said, 'you have just used the words "inadvertently" and "impression" and I must tell you that, in this context, I do not like them. I was married for many years to a master of the art of inadvertent impressions, and while I have no strong feelings either way on divorce – except to say that it is probably tidier than separation – I do like to know exactly where I stand. I am also a stickler for the truth. I hope that you will remember this in future.'

He was still digesting this information when we heard the front door open. To my relief, it was not Albert's enraged wife who erupted into the room but a cross-looking young woman with a silent ginger youth in tow.

'Johanna, this is my daughter, Norah,' said Albert, 'and her boyfriend, Kevin.'

Norah eyed me narrowly. 'Well, I'm sorry you've got

company,' she said, 'but there's no way we can watch *Culture Creep* next door now that you've gone and upset Mum.'

Even I had heard of *Culture Creep*: it was a new and peculiarly nasty reality TV show, beloved, it seemed, by everyone under the age of forty, including my own children. I think the idea was to bring together an interesting cross section of the different cultures in society, but in my opinion all it managed to prove was that every culture has its fair share of creeps. Norah walked past her father and switched on a large television in the corner of the kitchen. The demented sound of the *Culture Creep* audience baying for blood filled the room, but at least it drowned out the noise from next door.

Then the door opened again and a second refugee appeared. This one was small and plump with curtains of dark hair and a sorrowful expression.

'She's just broken Granny's tureen,' she said.

'Oh God,' said Albert. 'That was Sèvres!'

'I'm Rosie.' The newcomer looked at me with marginally more interest than her sister had shown. 'Sorry to crash your evening like this, but it's getting dangerous at home!' She rolled her eyes, then gave me a knowing little grin to let me know she wasn't the least bit sorry before plonking herself down next to her sister.

I waited for Albert to tell them that it was hard luck but he had his own evening planned, and they could all just take themselves off again, but he didn't. Instead, he stood there looking like a man who had unexpectedly found himself between a tiger and a pride of lions and was wondering how on earth to get away unscathed.

And it occurred to me suddenly that I might be underestimating the unseen Carmel: quite possibly she wasn't deranged at all, just creating havoc in order to drive her children next door. After all, what surer way to ruin Albert's chances of a night of passion? The more I thought about it, the more likely it seemed. Whatever the truth of the matter, there didn't seem much hope of rescuing the evening.

'Don't worry,' I said. 'I was just going anyway,' and abandoning my wine, I left. Of course it was only when I was outside that I remembered that I didn't have my own car, but Albert had hurried after me, and drove me home.

It was a silent journey: I was adjusting my expectations of being welcomed into the bosom of Albert's family, while Albert was probably hoping that least said would be soonest mended – or, at any rate, forgotten.

The road home from Belfast winds down the coast to the seaside town of Bangor. On the way are Holywood and the leafy suburbs of Helen's Bay, Carnalea and Crawfordsburn. There are golf courses, picturesque inns and a country park with delightful walks. By day the colours of the lough change with the weather, and there is a never-ending procession of cargo ships and ferries going to and fro.

Just after Holywood, we turned down to Seapark. On

high summer weekends and evenings the lawns and paths are crowded, but on a cold moonlit night there is often no one there at all, and it is as good a place as any for some quiet reflection. Albert and I stood for some time at the edge of the water, looking out at the lights on the other side of the lough, as we listened to the soothing suck and hiss of the sea.

Eventually my silence wore him down and he was forced to speak. 'Johanna,' he said, 'I am so sorry for the unfortunate way the evening has turned out. I realise I didn't manage things very well, but perhaps we could talk about it all another day?'

He sounded so weary that I turned and took him in my arms. I kissed him and told him not to worry: I said I was sure it would all be all right in the end, and at the time, I believed that. Then I suggested that we go home to my blessedly child-free sanctuary and open another bottle of wine. So that is what we did, and the evening ended in a most satisfactory manner after all.

Chapter 4

The next week was a busy one. As well as my three days at Archibald's, I sometimes helped out on a Friday afternoon at the Good Intentions Bookshop. This particular week Dolores was away, having twisted an ankle while walking in the Mournes, and her temporary absence from work had caused a surge in custom: the tougher customers felt they had a better chance of picking up a bargain – or of browbeating the staff into a discount – but most of the regulars simply felt safer when Dolores wasn't there.

Sybilla, having roped me in to help, had gone home to take Percy to the vet (a case of suspected claw rot – or something) and had left me with Basil, an eighty-year-old whose interests were bee-keeping and opera. According to Good Intentions policy, therefore, he was in charge of keeping those sections of the shop in order. As there were rarely any books on either subject, his duties were light, and he spent most of his time fiddling with the radio to ensure that both programme and volume met his particular requirements.

When I arrived, the powerful sound of *Götterdämmerung* was rending the air and Basil was gazing with a perplexed expression at the till, while a small but restive queue of customers waited to be served.

'Ah, Johanna, we seem to have a slight problem: it says the total is £2,001.50. That can't be right.'

'It should be £3.50,' said the customer indignantly. 'This one's £2 and this one's £1.50. How difficult is that?'

Luckily, Wagnerian crescendos drowned out the rest of his comments on Basil's diminishing brain cells, but after him came a ferrety-looking woman who did her best to take advantage of the situation.

'Would you take 50p for this one, love?' She was holding out a shiny, new and very clearly priced paperback. 'I'm just a wee pensioner, you know.'

Fortunately I had once seen Dolores deal with exactly this request: 'Do you think this is a charity?' she had asked indignantly. And when the customer had had the temerity to answer yes, Dolores had replied, 'Not for you it isn't,' and whipped the book out of his hands. So with this sterling example in mind, I held my ground.

'I'm a wee pensioner myself,' I said, 'but we must all do our bit to help those less fortunate than ourselves. That will be £2.50. Thank you.'

She scuttled off, muttering darkly. When I had dealt with

the rest of the people in the queue, I turned my attention to sorting out the till. Most of the Good Intentions volunteers had worked in the shop for years but they were still alarmed, and all too often bamboozled, by the workings of what they regarded as an infernal machine. And given fading eyesight and the fact that Northern Ireland has a bewildering variety of banknotes to cope with (not to mention a thriving business in forged ones), it is not surprising that the takings rarely tallied. At Archibald's Antiques the problem did not arise: we had no till. On the few occasions that anything was sold, the money was simply stuffed into a drawer, and only the most insistent customer was given a receipt. Or change.

Now, you might well wonder how an establishment such as Archibald's could afford an assistant, even a poorly paid one working for just three days a week. The answer is that it was never a business – it was a hobby. It was also a convenient cover.

I first met Archibald Minor a few months after my return to Northern Ireland. I had no car at the time, and very little money, so my chief source of pleasure was a weekly bus trip to some town or village chosen at random from the map, where I would explore the churches, second-hand shops and markets, and eat my sandwiches in a park, or – surreptitiously – with a cup of coffee in a cafe. On one such journey I found myself in Saintfield, a charming village on the road between Belfast and Downpatrick, and there, in a little shop that sold antiques and second-hand books, I fell into conversation with the two delightful men who owned the business.

I had remarked on a pair of handsome red volumes entitled *With the Flag to Pretoria*: the proprietors, it transpired, had a great interest in military history and had visited South Africa some years before. When I confessed that I had been born in Pretoria, they insisted on giving me tea and showing me other treasures. An hour later, clutching a little copy of *The Hunting of the Snark* (awarded in 1935 to Agnes Tomb, for Diligence), I took my leave, but as I turned to go I said, 'What a pity you don't need an assistant – I would love to work in a shop like this!'

It was meant as a compliment rather than a plea for employment, but a large man who had just come in, removed his hat, and gave me an old-fashioned bow.

'I have a shop in Belfast,' he said, 'and I am looking for a part-time assistant. Perhaps you would care to call on me?' And he handed me a card on which were engraved the words 'Archibald's Antiques'.

And that was how I came to work for Archie. He was a deeply mysterious man – he lived above the shop in a flat to which no one was ever invited and was devoted only to the ungrateful Morris. (I am a cat lover myself but I harbour no misconceptions about the species, and Morris was, even for a cat, singularly self-absorbed.) Archie couldn't afford to pay much, but I was happy with our arrangement: I kept an eye on both shop and cat, in return for which I had a small but adequate salary and a warm, quiet place in which to read, largely undisturbed by customers. Archie was mostly absent, driving around the countryside in search of antiques, or so I assumed.

In the beginning I worried about the dearth of customers, but gradually I realised that selling things was not the aim of Archie's enterprise. The shop was Archie's plaything, a repository for his toys, and a place where, on Fridays and Saturdays, he entertained his friends – mild, like-minded men who collected stamps, coins, medals and ancient postcards. And whatever Archie had done in his previous existence, it seemed to have provided sufficiently for his retirement.

He was resolutely private. By the end of the first year I knew only that he played bridge twice a week, was a member of various historical preservation societies and that he had a sister in Australia. Apart from that, I knew nothing about him. Even Dolores, whom I suspected of keeping dossiers on everyone in the street, could tell me nothing more. And then, halfway through my second year working for him, I discovered Archie's secret. What happened was that one evening he came upon me in the shop, twenty minutes after I should have left, and found me crying.

'Good heavens, Johanna! What has happened? Are you ill?'

In his consternation, he put the package he was carrying on the desk and fished in his pocket for a handkerchief. It was red silk and clearly not intended for the blowing of noses but I took it anyway.

'I'm sorry, Archie.' Sniff. 'No, I'm not ill. It's just … it's my birthday … '

Archie looked at me keenly. 'And you have nothing planned? No lover waiting with an armful of roses? None of your children at home?'

I shook my head and snuffled some more.

'Well then, Johanna, I should be very honoured if you would allow me to invite you to dinner. It will do my reputation no end of good to be seen with such a decorative woman.'

'Oh, Archie,' I cried, and threw my arms around him – and in so doing knocked his package to the ground, where it split open to reveal multiple copies of a very lurid-looking book.

I was instantly diverted. 'Archie!' I exclaimed. '*Milord Demon* by Cecilia MacBride. I'm amazed! Who would have thought that you were a fan of Cecilia MacBride?' I paused. 'But why have you got ten copies of the same book? Are you giving them away as Christmas presents?'

Archie had gone purple. 'Good God, Johanna! I certainly don't read them and I wouldn't dream of giving them away… it's just that they always send ten copies … ' He stopped in some confusion, but I could see a letter lying on top of them, and the heading was that of a well-known publisher. Slowly, light began to dawn.

'You didn't *write* them, did you?'

Archie clutched his head and groaned.

'*You're* Cecilia MacBride?' I was thunderstruck. 'Good lord,

Archie – I can hardly believe it!'

Archie was looking as mortified as it is possible for a man to look – and no wonder. I hadn't read Cecilia MacBride myself, but I had certainly heard of her, as the author of what can most politely be described as historical erotica.

'But, Archie,' I said, 'how on earth did you come to come to be Cecilia MacBride?'

He gave a helpless shrug. 'I started out as a journalist, you know, but I always liked historical novels: I used to read my mother's collection of Georgette Heyer when I was a boy. And then, one day, it occurred to me that there might be a market for something along the same lines but a bit … racier.'

'Well, from all accounts you've certainly managed that,' I said. 'I can't wait to read one for myself.'

'Johanna, I beg you not to!' Archie's face contorted with distress.

'Oh, all right. I probably wouldn't dare be seen with it anyway. Dolores had one in the bookshop last week: she threw it out. Pure filth, she said.'

'She's right,' said Archie, 'but it does provide me with a very useful income. And now that you know the awful truth, do you mind if we eat in? I was planning a little celebration anyway and it would be rather nice to have company for a change. I have a meal all ready to heat and a bottle of rather good wine.'

Which is how I found myself following Archie and Morris upstairs and into a most luxurious living room which was lined from floor to ceiling with the myriad titles, editions and translations of the collected works of the world-famous, and enormously successful, Cecilia MacBride.

We ate at a round table in the bay window. 'This is delicious, Archie,' I said, spooning up the casserole. 'Don't tell me you made it yourself?'

'Marks & Spencer,' said Archie. 'Have some more wine.'

I held out my glass: it was a long time since I'd had wine that good.

'I can see why you don't ask anyone up.' I gazed at the surrounding books. 'The cat would be out of the bag immediately.'

'Indeed,' said Archie. 'And imagine what that would do to my reputation. I should have to resign from the bridge club.'

This was such a shattering thought that it silenced us both. Then Archie gave a little cough. 'I do hope, Johanna, that I can rely on your discretion?'

'You have my word on it,' I replied. 'But I rather think, dear Archie, that the time has come to discuss the question of my salary.'

'Johanna,' said Archie, leaning back in his chair and raising his glass to me, 'I salute you! I knew the moment I set eyes on you that you were a formidable woman. What a pity I can only love Morris!'

Given the sort of thing that was reputed to go on in Archie's books, I thought it was probably a good thing that his passion was confined to cats, but I didn't say so.

Instead I raised my own glass and drank to our continuing good fortune.

And, of course, if I hadn't been working for Archie, I might never have spent so many hours in Good Intentions, or encountered Albert. And if he and I had not been brought together by M. Heaney's *The Traveller's Guide to Ancient County Down*, we would not have embarked on our outings together. As my sister Frederika (known to my children as Auntie Fruitloop) would say, 'The way may twist and turn, but in the end, all things are connected.' Or something like that.

Chapter 5

Not long after my ill-starred visit to Chestnut Avenue, Albert and I set out one Sunday morning in search of the Goward Dolmen. The rain, which had been falling for weeks, showed signs at last of letting up at last, and I had planned another picnic. I was eager to visit other sites in the guide to County Down, of course, but I also wanted an opportunity to discuss the future. I have often found that potentially difficult conversations can be more easily conducted in the open air: there is something inherently calming about the great outdoors, and there is less danger to breakable property – a fact that I felt Carmel Morrow would do well to consider.

Ever since our first meeting, Albert and I had been engaged in a continuous and delightful conversation – on the phone, by email, in bed. It was one of Albert's many charms that he actively enjoyed rambling conversations in the middle of the night. We had discussed books, music, politics and our love for one another at length, but I could not help feeling that there were other matters that needed to be addressed.

Spring had been the air all week, together with a noticeable perking-up of the winter-worn populace. Upstairs, Sticky Wicket had embarked on his annual DIY frenzy, and on his way in and out with parcels from B&Q he had more than once buttonholed Albert for discussion of the summer's cricketing prospects. It was the tail end of one of these conversations that I caught as I emerged from my flat with the picnic basket.

'South Africa is in good form,' Sticky Wicket was saying, 'and our very own South African too, if you don't mind my saying so, old man. Never seen such a change in a woman – been positively civil to me lately! Mind you, she still scares the living daylights out of me. Oh hello, Johanna – got a good picnic there, have you?' He gazed hungrily at the basket as I handed it to Albert.

'Quails' eggs,' I said, 'champagne, smoked salmon, Parma ham, melon and a lovely ripe Camembert. Oh, and a few chocolate truffles and hothouse grapes.' In fact it contained an unusually frugal selection of cold meats, salad, crusty bread and Cheddar, but he deserved to suffer. 'Have a nice day, Sticky Wicket!'

'Johanna, my love,' said Albert, as we drove off, 'why are you so unkind to that poor man? He's terrified of you.'

'Good,' I replied. 'It will keep him in his place.' But I could see that an explanation was called for.

'When I first moved in, Albert, I was always coming home to

find him in my flat, doing so-called repairs, and he was forever turning up at mealtimes.' I did my best to mimic Sticky's plummy tones: '*Oh gosh, Johanna, that does smell delicious. I'm only having an egg and toast myself.* Or he'd be knocking on my door late at night to ask if I had any aspirin. It was quite obvious what he was after. In the end I had to be very firm. I went to him and said, Mr Wicket – that's his actual name, you know, Sidney Wicket – Mr Wicket, you are giving me a problem, or to use a cricketing metaphor you will understand, I find myself presented with a Sticky Wicket. You are my landlord and I am your tenant and that is as far as this relationship is ever going to go. I do not expect you to knock on my door again unless it is an emergency, or to enter my flat unless expressly invited to do so. Do I make myself clear? And I am glad to say that after that I had no more trouble.'

'I'm not surprised,' said Albert. 'Mind you, I can't help feeling sorry for him. If I'd been your landlord, I'd have knocked on your door as well.'

'If you'd been my landlord, I'd have let you in.' I reached out a hand to pat his thigh and then quickly removed it as the car swerved into oncoming traffic. 'Now, concentrate, dear Albert: we must take the next left turn.'

We were heading for Castlewellan. After studying the map with care, I had thought that we might, en route, take in Slieve Croob, but it turned out to be remarkably elusive. It is one of those mountains that approached from the wrong direction will loom first on your left and then on your right; it will appear straight ahead one minute, and the next minute be shrinking in your rear-view mirror. On this occasion it finally disappeared completely into a canopy of cloud, so we gave up and made for Castlewellan, a village with a wide main street, chestnut-lined squares and a beautifully kept country park. The park is famous for its mile-long lake and extraordinary variety of trees and shrubs, but on this particular Sunday we did not stop. Instead we followed the road to Newry for a couple of miles until we spotted a reservoir on the right, and a left-hand turning up a lane, to the Drumena Cashel and Souterrain.

A narrow opening in the thick dry-stone wall led us into the grassy enclosure of the cashel. Like so many of these places, it felt immensely peaceful and untroubled by the outside world. There was no one else there and no sound but birdcalls and the wind. Situated as it is on the northern slopes of the Mournes, there are sweeping views to the south across the valley and a small lough, and an opening in the ground with steps leading down into a souterrain. It had been restored well, and although the ancient inhabitants who might have sheltered there were probably a good deal shorter than Albert, there was ample room for us to traverse its length. I have a photo of Albert's shining dome emerging at the other end to prove it.

From the Drumena Cashel we continued in the direction of Hilltown until we saw the Goward Road signposted on our left. More lane than road, it twisted and turned for nearly a mile, and quickly deteriorated into a bumpy track, but the journey was worth the trouble, because the Goward Dolmen took our breath away.

We came upon it quite suddenly – it was tucked away, as M. Heaney had promised, on the downward slope below the lane. It was extraordinarily impressive, with an immense granite capstone, at least thirteen feet long and nearly as wide, supported by pillar stones almost six feet in height, and beyond it, there were panoramic views to the north.

As fitful sunlight came and went, I photographed the dolmen from every angle; then we spread our rug on the grass and unpacked our picnic. We ate, we drank, and Albert leaned back against the ancient stones while I leaned back against Albert. It was one of those fleeting times of intense and silent happiness.

Then a little wintry gust of wind – or possibly a Neolithic ghost breathing down my neck – caused me to shiver. Albert tightened his arms.

'Are you cold, my darling?'

'Not really, but the sun won't last much longer – those clouds are building. And speaking of clouds on the horizon, I've been meaning to ask you: have you talked to any of your family about what happened the other night?'

'Well, yes and no. That is to say, I haven't seen much of Norah – she and Kevin have been in Donegal – but Rosie did ask me if you were my girlfriend.'

'And what did you say?'

'I said you were. And that I hoped you would all get to know each other better. In time.'

'Hmm,' I said.

'Johanna, my love,' Albert stroked my hair, 'you mustn't worry: I promise you it will all work out in the end.'

'I certainly hope so,' I replied, 'but we are no longer young and I do not feel that time is on our side. I must be honest, Albert, and tell you that I cannot help but feel that a man who left his wife five years ago but only got as far as the house next door has not entirely detached himself. And while you are always welcome in my house, I certainly don't feel welcome in yours. Perhaps, my love, the time has come to reconsider your position?'

There was silence. Then Albert sighed.

'I know you're right, Johanna, and changes must be made. But if you can be patient just a little longer, I'd like to manage it in a way that will cause as little hurt as possible, especially to Norah and Rosie. You know how difficult these things are, my darling, you have children ... '

'Indeed I do,' I replied. 'Four of them, and I do not expect any one of them to live next door – because, like yours, they are all grown up.'

Luckily for Albert an enormous cloud engulfed the sun just then and a sharp spattering of rain sent us scrambling for the safety of the car. By the time we turned back on to the main road, it was coming down in torrents.

On a clear day the descent into Rostrevor is glorious, with Carlingford Lough spread out before you, and if the weather had held we might have continued in the direction of Newcastle. As it was, we turned right, to Warrenpoint, and on to Newry and Belfast, cocooned in our separate thoughts, and the driving sheets of rain.

Albert didn't come in with me when we got back: he had the beginnings of a headache, he said – the onset of a chill, perhaps – and although I suspected it was probably due to anxiety at the prospect of further upheavals in his life, I felt contrite.

'Go home,' I said, 'and tuck yourself up with a hot-water bottle, and I'm sorry if I upset you – it's just that I cannot bear any skulking around. I love you so much, but I want our relationship to be open and honest, and fair to us both.'

Then I kissed him tenderly and went inside to heat up the stew I had planned to share with him. But even before the meal was ready – just as I poured a glass of good South African Pinotage to accompany it – my telephone rang.

I was expecting a call from Finn, my eldest son, who had left a message for me earlier, and it was also the time of day that my daughter Ellie tended to phone, so I went to answer it eagerly. But it was neither Finn nor Ellie.

'Is that Johanna?' a female voice enquired. 'This is Norah Morrow, Albert's daughter.'

My stomach dropped as I envisaged disaster: a car crash, a heart attack brought on by stress … but it was none of these.

'Sorry to bother you,' she said, 'but I found your number next to the phone and I wondered if my father was with you?'

'He left ten minutes ago,' I replied. 'Is something wrong?'

'Oh no, it's just that we expected him back a bit earlier – it's Mum's birthday and we're waiting for him to be take us out for dinner.'

'Well I'm sure he'll be there any minute now,' I said. 'Enjoy your evening.'

I replaced the receiver and drank the wine in one gulp – then I hurled the glass with a force that even Carmel Morrow might have envied into Sticky Wicket's tastefully tiled fireplace.

Chapter 6

✉ From: johannavanheerden@hotmail.com
   To: aj.morrow@googlemail.co.uk

Dear Albert,
I am not sure what I feel about the man
I love taking his estranged wife out to
dinner, but what I *am* sure of is that I
object to being deceived. If you have
other arrangements it is better to say so
at the start rather than to pretend to
be ill. Sticky Wicket is scratching at
my door. I think I might let him in to
console me.
Johanna

✉ From: aj.morrow@googlemail.co.uk
   To: johannavanheerden@hotmail.com

My darling Johanna,
I am so very sorry. The girls had
arranged the dinner and I didn't want

to disappoint them but I knew it would
make you unhappy and I couldn't bear to
distress you. I should have told you. If
it is any comfort, it was not a success:
the food was poor and Carmel threatened
to hit the waiter. I wished the whole
time that I had been with you.
Please forgive me – or at least let me
see you tomorrow so that I can plead my
case. And for God's sake don't let Sticky
Wicket in.
Your loving (if unloved)
Albert

✉ From: johannavanheerden@hotmail.com
To: aj.morrow@googlemail.co.uk

Coffee. Tomorrow. 11 a.m. at Archie's.
And I expect you to grovel.
Johanna

✉ From: aj.morrow@googlemail.co.uk
To: johannavanheerden@hotmail.com

I will be there on the dot, on my knees.
And if you will let me, I will take you
to lunch. And to dinner. And to Paris in
the spring ... you beautiful thing.
Love,
Albert xxxx

Of course, there were other emails flying back and forth, as I later discovered.

✉ From: ellie3os@hotmail.com
  To: fingarden@hotmail.com

  Finn, why don't you ever answer your
  phone? I've been trying to get hold of
  you for days.
  Ellie

✉ From: fingarden@hotmail.com
  To: ellie3os@hotmail.com

  Hi Ellie, sorry, we've been a bit busy
  and I lost my phone. What's all this about
  our ma falling in love? She hasn't said
  anything to me. We're going to Marta's
  family for Easter so I'm not likely to
  see her for a while. I wouldn't worry
  about her though: he's hardly likely to
  be after her money! When are you coming
  home yourself? Marta and Pip say hi.
  Love from me,
  Finn

✉ From: ellie3os@hotmail.com
  To: nualavanshea@gmail.co.uk

  Hi Nuala-pie. Did you know Ma was seeing

someone? I think you and Seamus should go over at Easter and report back. I've had some very strange emails lately: it could just be senility but I suspect it's Love.

✉ From: nualavanshea@gmail.co.uk
   To: ellie3os@hotmail.com

   What, you mean like a mad passionate affair?

✉ From: ellie3os@hotmail.com
   To: nualavanshea@gmail.co.uk

   Yes

✉ From: nualavanshea@gmail.com
   To: ellie3os@hotmail.com

   Ew!

Chapter 7

Downpatrick is the county town of Down and boasts two famous hills: one is the Mound of Down, site of an ancient Ulster stronghold; the other is the Hill of Down, where a large stone in the churchyard of the Church of Ireland cathedral is said to mark Saint Patrick's burial place – although this, like so much else in Northern Ireland, is disputed. What cannot be denied is the commanding position of the cathedral itself: long before the town comes into view, the traveller approaching from the north will see its twin spires, as sharp and uncompromising as the pricked ears of a Dobermann on guard.

Some time between St Patrick's Day and Easter, Albert and I drove directly to Downpatrick from Belfast, stopping just before the town itself to see the ruins of Inch Abbey. This is another ancient site – according to M. Heaney there was a monastery here by 800 AD – but the Gothic remains, which have been most beautifully restored, are of a later Cistercian abbey. There were one or two other people wandering, like us, between the grey stone walls and arches, and across the springing grass that sloped down to the edge of a little lake, but we had a wooden bench to ourselves, with a view of the ruins, and beyond them, trees and hills, and sunlit water.

I lifted my face to the sun and sighed with pleasure. 'How lovely it is to be able to sit outside again and feel the sun. It's one of the things I miss so much, just being outside and feeling warm.'

'Do you get very homesick?' Albert sounded worried.

'Not as much as I used to.' I squeezed his hand. 'But I haven't been home for a couple of years, and I've been thinking I should make a trip back soon.'

'Do you plan to be away for long?'

'A couple of weeks, perhaps. It's too far to go for less.'

A solitary magpie landed a few feet away. A moment later it was joined by another. One for sorrow, two for joy, I thought.

Albert cleared his throat. 'I don't suppose you would consider letting me come with you?'

'Oh, Albert, nothing would make me happier!' I flung my arms around him. 'I so badly want you to meet all my family – especially Frederika – and besides, I don't really think I could bear to go without you.'

'I'm delighted to hear it,' Albert replied, and scandalised a passing couple of twenty-somethings by returning my embrace with unseemly enthusiasm.

From Inch Abbey we went on to Downpatrick, where the steeply climbing Mall leads up to a museum, housed in an eighteenth-century gaol. We wandered happily through it and through the unusually small and charming cathedral, and then went back into the ancient town, which we planned to explore further – until a sudden shower of rain drove us to abandon cultural pursuits in favour of a pub with a glorious peat fire.

'Johanna,' said Albert, some time later, 'very few things give me as much pleasure as seeing the way you can clear a plate, but sometimes I can't help wondering if you went hungry as a child?'

'Not if I was quick,' I replied, as I spooned up the last buttery juices of my salmon. 'There were a lot of us. And that reminds me: have you made any plans for Easter?'

Albert, who had been gazing at me fondly, immediately looked stricken. 'Ah, well, I've been meaning to talk to you about it … the thing is, Johanna, I have a cousin I don't see very often who will be over from Canada with her daughters, and Carmel has gone and invited everyone for lunch on Easter Sunday. They have a very busy schedule so it would be a chance to see them all at once, but– '

I reached out a slightly buttery finger and laid it gently on his lips. 'It's fine, Albert. As it happens, I'm having lunch with Socrates: the twins are coming home for Easter and he has invited us all out – and the opportunity to get Socrates to pay for a slap-up meal is such a rarity that I couldn't bring myself to turn it down.'

'Socrates?' Albert looked stunned. 'I thought you'd left him somewhere in Africa.'

'I did. But it turns out he's been living in Dublin for a while and as he is putting himself up in luxury while he's here, it appears that whatever he's up to, it has been successful. Criminal, probably, but lucrative.' I drained the last of my Sauvignon Blanc. 'Anyway, Nuala and Seamus are going back down to Dublin with him after Easter, but I do want you to meet them, so I thought we might have a picnic on Easter Monday?'

'With Socrates?' Albert looked horrified.

'Certainly not. He has dodgy relatives he can visit. Just you, me and the twins.'

'I'd be delighted,' said Albert. 'And now, my darling, what's next – the St Patrick's Centre, or the Ballynoe Stone Circle – or both?'

The Ballynoe Stone Circle lies south of Downpatrick, just off the road to Killough. As usual, M. Heaney's directions and description turned out to be exact. It was indeed a gentle and unusual site, accessed by a long, upward-sloping lane arched by thorn trees, which give a fairy-like atmosphere to the place. The outer circle, 108 feet in diameter, is made up of large stones, some more than six feet tall. There are smaller stones and a cairn within, and wonderful sweeping views of the surrounding countryside. On the day that we were there, a herd of cows grazed peacefully around us and away to the southwest – now that the rain had stopped – the Mournes were clearly visible.

We leaned against each other and drank in the tranquillity and beauty of the place.

'Look,' said Albert. 'See how the hawthorn is beginning to bud. The blossom will be out in May.'

It was Albert who told me that fairy thorns are never cut, for fear of bringing bad luck. You will see them often, in the middle of a field, with plough marks all around but the tree untouched. And perhaps it was the magic of the thorn trees that made Albert take both my hands in his just then.

'Johanna, my darling, we'll come back in May to see the blossom, and we'll go to Paris, and to South Africa too! And by autumn I hope the house will be sold, and you and I will have found somewhere to live together.'

I had to squeeze my eyes shut against the tears as I put my arms around him and hugged him fiercely. I could see us clearly, snug in a warm interior, with snow outside and a Christmas tree in the window, mulled wine steaming gently … then I opened my eyes, and froze.

'Albert,' I whispered, 'I think one of those cows is a bull!'

Fortunately Albert was a countryman born and bred, and he knew just what to do. We retreated, slowly but steadily, with Albert placing himself between the bull and me, until we were close enough to the entrance to the lane to sprint for safety. But it was a cautionary experience, and the traveller in rural Ireland will be well advised to look carefully before venturing into unknown territory.

There is another unusually large stone circle much closer to Belfast: this is the Giant's Ring, and is the only prehistoric site that I visited without Albert. The ring itself is an enormous bank of earth and stones lying in a bend of the river Lagan, and is the largest ritual enclosure in the country. There is a dolmen in the centre, and according to M. Heaney the chamber once contained fragments of cremated bone, but otherwise the history of the place remains a mystery.

My reason for being there, later that year, was that one of the Good Intentions volunteers lived in the area, and had invited me to tea. She had spent her childhood in South Africa, so we passed a pleasant afternoon reminiscing over scones and homemade jam. Agnes was a tiny, energetic woman with strong opinions who shared her house with half a dozen cats, and fed several other cats and dogs in the neighbourhood, as well as two donkeys in a field across the way, and such birds as had the wit to avoid the cats.

Just I was about to leave, a young man whom I had taken for a gardener, approached us and was introduced by Agnes as her nephew, Marc.

He dusted off his hands to shake mine, then pointed to the shrubbery where he had been working. 'I think I've cut those bushes back enough, Aunt Agnes,' he said, 'but if you don't mind I won't stay for tea – I need to be getting back into town to collect my car before the garage closes.'

'Can I give you a lift anywhere?' I offered. 'I'm heading back through town myself.'

And that was how I came to be driving him back down the lane, and happened to mention as I did so that I had visited the Giant's Ring on my way to call on his aunt.

'I know it well,' Marc replied. 'In fact I've done quite a lot of research there.'

'Oh? Are you an archaeologist?'

'I'm a history teacher. But some years ago I wrote a guide to the ancient sites of County Down.'

I very nearly swerved into a ditch. 'You're never M. Heaney!'

'Yes I am. Marc Heaney. I can't believe you've read my book.'

'Book?' I said. 'It is my *bible*!' And I explained how Albert and I had been following in his footsteps. 'But I'm amazed that you're so young: I imagined you as a hoary old academic, if not dead! Tell me, have you written any other books?'

'Funny you should ask,' he replied. 'I've spent the last few years working on a guide to ancient County Antrim, and with a bit of luck it will be published fairly soon.'

All this was later in the year of course. At the time of our visit to the Ballynoe Stone Circle, it had never occurred to me that my path might one day cross M. Heaney's, but as my sister Frederika would say, 'All things are intertwined in celestial harmony.'

It is something I frequently have difficulty remembering.

Chapter 8

Celestial harmony was not immediately apparent at Easter. Seamus and Nuala had arrived a day earlier than expected, with a great quantity of washing and a small striped cat. I found one sitting on my kitchen table and the other spread all over the floor.

'Good God,' I said. 'What on earth is all this?'

'Sorry,' said Seamus. 'Our machine broke down last week.'

'And are there no launderettes in Glasgow?' I enquired. 'But never mind the washing, what is that cat doing on my table?'

'That's Tiger Lily,' said Nuala. 'We couldn't leave her behind – there was no one to look after her.'

The twins take after my Dutch forebears: they are tall and blonde and remarkably alike – a resemblance which, despite all my efforts to emphasise their separate identities, they have carefully fostered. I looked at them now and sighed. Identical skinny black clothing and sphinx-like expressions. Ellie says they are unnatural but Finn maintains that it was having to stand up to their elder sister that caused them to bond so firmly in the first place. Whatever the cause, they are inseparable.

I reached out a hand to Tiger Lily, who rubbed her head against my arm and purred loudly. 'Where did you get her?' I asked, softening in spite of myself.

'We found her in a skip,' said Seamus.

'She was starving,' said Nuala, 'poor little thing.'

'Well,' I said, 'you had better start putting your washing into the machine and then you can go down to the shops and buy cat food and a litter tray. And flea drops. I suppose you're expecting me to look after her while you're in Dublin with your father?'

They draped themselves around me, one on either side. I could feel them smirking at each other over my head.

'Well, just so long as you understand that she can't stay here a moment longer,' I said feebly. 'There's a clause in my lease that clearly states no pets. We'll have to keep her out of Sticky Wicket's sight.'

'Oh he's seen her already,' said Nuala. 'She stuck her head out of Seamus's pocket when we arrived. Seamus told him she plays cricket with a ping-pong ball. He fell in love immediately.'

'And does she?' I asked. 'Play cricket, I mean.'

'No idea,' my son replied.

'Seamus,' I said, 'there are times when you are worryingly like your father.'

*

This exchange took place on Thursday. On Friday morning I woke to find Tiger Lily curled in the crook of my neck and purring softly into my right ear.

'No,' I said firmly. 'I have too many problematic relationships as it is: I am not entering into one with you.'

But over the next two days I weakened. She was an extraordinarily endearing little cat, and she did indeed turn out to have a knack for cricket. The twins would position her on a table or sofa, then bowl her a ping-pong ball, which she unerringly batted to the far corners of the room. Sticky Wicket was invited down to watch, and roared with joy. He was also invited by Nuala to join our Sunday morning egg hunt.

'I'm sure you've got better things to do,' I said discouragingly.

'Not a bit of it,' said Sticky. 'Nothing I'd like more!'

I glared at all three of them but was prevented from further comment by the ringing of my phone. In the nature of one irritation following another, it was Socrates.

'Johanna? How are you? Look, I know this is short notice but I'm afraid I'm not going to make it to Belfast tomorrow: something urgent has come up and I'm going to have to stay in Dublin for the weekend. So, much as I'd like to, it doesn't look as though I'll be able to join you for lunch after all.'

'I am very well, thank you Socrates,' I responded. 'I won't ask you what has "come up" because it's probably something I'd rather not know about, but I would just like to point out that you weren't joining us – we were joining you. At your expense, or so I understood.'

'Ah yes, well, why don't you take Nuala and Seamus out somewhere nice and I'll reimburse you?'

I did not reply. The chances of there being somewhere nice for Easter Sunday lunch that hadn't been booked out weeks ago were slim; the chances of Socrates reimbursing me were even slimmer.

'Johanna? Are you still there? Now, don't be cross: you know I wouldn't let you down if I could possibly avoid it.' (I snorted.) 'I'll pick the twins up on Tuesday morning. You can tell them I've rented a dream cottage in Donegal.'

'Donegal? Not Dublin?'

'Change of plan,' said Socrates. 'I tell you what, why don't you come with us? I've been thinking lately that it's about time we both let bygones be bygones. What do you say?'

'Which particular bygones did you have in mind, Socrates? Are we talking about tax evasion, fraud and dodgy business deals too numerous to mention? Or possibly the involvement of my unsuspecting family in your vintage wine scam? For which, in case you have forgotten, you still owe my brother Stefanus rather a lot of money. Or, let me see – what about the time you were supposed to be sitting at your ailing granny's bedside when you were actually on a hunting trip and somehow ended up in jail? Where, with hindsight, I should have left you.' I paused for breath. 'Or are we just talking about your total failure ever to acknowledge or apologise for the endless trouble you caused?'

'Johanna,' my ex-husband sounded reproachful, 'I don't know why you always have to cast these things up. You need to learn to put them behind you – after all, we all make mistakes, and whatever little problems we may have had, they're all in the past now.'

'As are you, Socrates,' I replied, and put down the phone with what I felt was commendable restraint.

Nuala and Seamus took the news with equanimity: long association with their father has accustomed them to frequent changes of plan, but it did occur to me to wonder why Socrates should suddenly have a yearning for my company.

'Anyway,' said Nuala, 'Donegal might turn out to be better than Dublin. As long as it doesn't rain the whole time, we should get some good pictures.'

The twins were in their final year at art college, and their work was closely concerned with their relationship. In earlier years they had won accolades for performance-painting, an activity that involved them standing, identically dressed, in front of two easels, while painting abstract portraits of each other. A later refinement, also much admired, dispensed with the clothing. Naively, I was relieved when they branched into photography and film.

At any rate, they were happy enough to spend Easter Sunday just with me, and in the end we had a surprisingly pleasant day. We had long conversations with Finn and Marta in London and Ellie in – I think – Peru. It poured with rain but the egg hunt was successfully conducted indoors, and I'd found some lamb in the freezer, which I roasted – and which Sticky Wicket somehow managed to end up sharing. The twins, for some reason, found him hilarious, and he did contribute some reasonably good wine; but when I felt that he had had quite enough lunch – not to mention coffee, chocolates and two glasses of plum brandy – I rose purposefully to my feet.

'We mustn't keep you any longer, Sticky Wicket,' I said. 'We've had more of you than we deserve already. Besides, I have family matters that I must discuss with my children. So thank you for sharing our day.' And I steered him firmly out the door. Then I sat down on the sofa with my feet up, a twin on either side and Tiger Lily on my lap, and for the rest of the afternoon we watched old movies and polished off the remaining wine and chocolates in companionable silence.

The rain that had set in on Easter Sunday continued through the night and I woke with a feeling of foreboding. After all, it is never easy to introduce one's adult children to a new love, and when the introduction has been planned as a picnic, inclement weather is not encouraging. Even less encouraging was the discovery that the ham intended for our lunch had been reduced overnight to a shadow of its former self. A couple of unwashed glasses and plates with crumbs and smears of mustard pointed to the twins having had a midnight snack, helped no doubt by Tiger Lily, who was asleep on a pile of clean laundry, her little tummy stretched tight as a drum and an expression of deep contentment on her face.

Still, there was a quiche in the fridge, as well as the remains of the lamb, and plenty of cheese and fruit: we might have to sit in the car staring out at the rain but we were unlikely to starve. And in a couple of hours' time I would see Albert, from whom I had been apart for the last four days. My heart lifted – and lifted even further, I am sorry to say, when I remembered that my children would be off to Donegal the next day, leaving me free to entertain my darling in the manner to which I had so happily become accustomed.

By the time we set off the rain had also lifted and from the top of the Holywood Hills we could see the Mournes quite clearly, so we stuck to our original plan, which was to drive straight to Newcastle and on down the coast.

We stopped briefly at Dundrum, where there is a wonderful ruined castle up on a hill overlooking Dundrum Bay, and where the twins climbed to the top of the thirteenth-century keep and took a great many photos at considerable risk to life and limb. And we stopped again just long enough for Albert to buy ice creams, having been tipped off by me that the way to my youngest children's hearts lay directly through their stomachs. In fact, Nuala and Seamus, who had begun by treating him with wary politeness, very soon relaxed, and Albert wooed them shamelessly: he asked them endless questions about their art, their lives, their memories of Africa; he stopped the car whenever there was something they wanted to photograph; and he was very careful to behave towards me with impeccable propriety.

I knew that Newcastle was a popular resort at the foot of the Mourne Mountains: apart from the beauty of its setting, it is home to the Royal County Down Golf Club as well as being famous for its forest parks and walking trails. So it was no surprise that, despite the rain, the town was packed with holidaymakers. We decided not to stop, instead continuing on down the coastal road, through the fishing villages of Annalong and Kilkeel, until, a few miles south-east of Rostrevor, we saw the sign to the Kilfeaghan Dolmen.

The dolmen is behind a farm: a path led us through the farmyard and down to an enormous capstone supported by partly hidden pillars. As if to reward us for our perseverance, the day had suddenly cleared, and in the spring sunshine the view from the southern slopes of the Mournes and out over Carlingford Lough was spectacular. But we didn't stay long: hunger drove us back to the car and on up a winding track to a small car park, which was miraculously empty, save for two cars whose occupants were probably hiking further up the mountain. And on the other side of a little stream, we found a perfect picnic site.

I produced the quiche and lamb, the cheese and fruit, but

it was Albert who outdid himself, with a whole roast chicken (from a well-known store, I was relieved to see – Albert's cooking skills were still a largely unknown quantity) and, from a cooler-bag, a bottle of champagne and chocolates.

'Good man!' said Seamus, as we held out our glasses to be filled; then he raised his own to us. 'Here's to champagne picnics!'

'To Mum and Albert,' echoed Nuala. 'And to many more picnics!'

'To Nuala and Seamus,' I responded. Toasts are a tradition in our family. 'To health and happiness!'

'And to Johanna,' concluded Albert, 'who brings such happiness to us all.'

The twins exchanged glances, while I tried not to look unsuitably besotted and busied myself instead with handing out food; but I *did* feel so brim-full of happiness that it was hard not to think of it as seeping out into everything around me. And who can blame me? It was a beautiful spring day on the slopes of the Mournes, beside me were two of my children, and I was both loved and in love. Who could have asked for more?

There were abandoned dwellings up there in the hills: after lunch, Nuala and Seamus took a great many photographs of these sad and picturesque ruins while Albert and I just wandered. We met one or two returning hikers but mostly we had the place to ourselves.

'Well done,' I said to Albert, as we watched Nuala below us taking shots of her brother's head emerging from crumbling window frames. 'You've got on with them like a house on fire.'

'It's been a pleasure,' said Albert. 'They're delightful. And very knowledgeable about film.'

They had discovered this mutual interest over lunch, and as we were all fans of art-house movies, a long and enjoyable conversation had ensued. Socrates, I remembered, had been a great movie-lover too, but he had preferred westerns, and – unsurprisingly – the sort of action movie where the charming and irresponsible hero gets away with murder.

'You'll miss them when they're gone,' Albert continued.

'Yes.' I squeezed his hand. 'It's been lovely having them around, but their father is collecting them in the morning so by teatime I shall be badly in need of consolation.'

'In that case,' said Albert, 'I'll be round by four o'clock.'

I might have known that Socrates would be late. He finally arrived at a quarter to four, and by the time I got Seamus and Nuala and their baggage out of the flat, Albert's gleaming head was just emerging from his car. Inevitably, Sticky Wicket had also materialised.

'Socrates – Albert – Sidney,' I said. I could see Albert bracing himself, and Socrates raising an eyebrow in a way I knew all too well, but we van Heerdens pride ourselves on our ability to deal with awkward situations, so I didn't give them any longer to size each other up.

'Sticky Wicket, be so kind as to take Albert inside and talk to him about cricket while I say goodbye to my children,' I commanded. Then I shoved Socrates firmly in the small of his back and propelled him and the twins down the path and out through the front gate. As I kissed my children and waved them off I reflected that the land-cruiser being driven by my ex-husband was a great deal newer and smarter than any car that I was ever likely to own; on the other hand it was a comfort to know that their transport, if not their father, was both reliable and safe.

Then I went back inside to rescue Albert from Sticky Wicket, and to resume my interrupted private life.

Chapter 9

✉ From: johannavanheerden@hotmail.com
   To: aj.morrow@googlemail.co.uk

I've just had a call from Nuala and
Seamus: apparently they aren't coming
back to Belfast tomorrow after all.
Socrates has business in Scotland so it's
easier for them to go straight to the
ferry with their father and get a lift
with him to Glasgow. It seems I have
inherited Tiger Lily!

✉ From: aj.morrow@googlemail.co.uk
   To: johannavanheerden@hotmail.com

Does this mean that you are free tomorrow
night?

✉ From: johannavanheerden@hotmail.com
   To: aj.morrow@googlemail.co.uk

We might be - if Tiger Lily has no other
plans.

✉ From: aj.morrow@googlemail.co.uk
   To: johannavanheerden@hotmail.com

Tell her I'll bring prawns - and a bottle
of champagne to celebrate. I have some
good news, darling.
Until tomorrow xxx

✉ From: johannavanheerden@hotmail.com
   To: cosmictraveller@yahoo.co.za

Frederika, why aren't you ever at home? I
have been trying to Skype you all day - I
have wonderful news: Albert has spoken
to an estate agent at last and his house
will be on the market by the end of this
month!! I am so happy and excited at the
thought that before long we will have
our own place, together - I have to keep
pinching myself to make sure
I'm not dreaming! Oh Freddy, I can't wait
for you to meet him. I know that you are
going to love him too. Ring me soon. I am
dying to talk.
Big hugs and kisses,
Johanna xx

✉ From: cosmictraveller@yahoo.co.za
To: johannavanheerden@hotmail.com

Hello Snoekie. Sorry, I was at the Kalk
Bay Moon Circle. Quite mind-blowing:
some extraordinary connections and
unexpected channels of communication.
Our most recent recruit, Thandi Magunda,
has turned out to be quite exceptionally
sensitive. I do have to tell you though
that Crystal Coetzee had a rather
worrying message from the other side:
an intimation of some sort of disaster,
possibly in Ireland. Still, it's probably
nothing to do with you and Albert.
Sleep tight, darling, and I'll talk to
you tomorrow.
Freddy xxx

✉ From: ellie3os@hotmail.com
To: nualavanshea@gmail.co.uk;
seamusvanshea@gmail.co.uk

Hi little brother and sister, I like the
photos. Glad you had such a good Easter
and that our mother's boyfriend met with
your approval – although it sounds to me
as though he bribed you with food and
drink. I don't know when I'm coming home:
Carlos wants to go to Brazil but there's

a possibility of a job in Chile. I'll try
to get back for Mum's birthday. How's the
film going? Does anyone wear clothes
in it? Be good.
Ellie xox

✉ From: johannavanheerden@hotmail.com
To: cosmictraveller@yahoo.co.za

Well, Crystal Coetzee turned out to be
right – possibly for the first time in
her life. Albert's house plans have been
put on hold because his daughter Rosie
is turning twenty-one in June and both
houses are going to be needed to put up
all the American and Canadian relatives
who are coming over for the party.
Apparently B&Bs won't do and For Sale
signs in the garden will cast gloom –
although nothing like the gloom that has
been cast on me! And we can't go to Paris
either because there is an Icelandic
volcano about to spread volcanic ash
everywhere and/or terrorist threats and
imminent air strikes: take your pick.
I haven't had the heart to mention
South Africa again either. To be honest
Freddy, I suspect that Albert might have
a fear of flying ... either that or cold

feet! Still, to make up for all this
disappointment we are going to the west
of Ireland, somewhere I have never been,
to a place called Achill Island, and we
are going next weekend – so if there are
any more intimations of doom, I don't
want to hear about them!
Johanna xx

✉ From: ellie3os@hotmail.co.uk
To: fingarden@hotmail.co.uk

Dear Finn,
Thanks for your advice about Chile but I
think we're going to Brazil after all.
We're looking into buses and trains at
the moment. But if I can find a cheap
flight I'll try to come home for Mum's
birthday – and I *am* worried about her:
she's gone off with this Albert to some
island off Mayo and she barely knows him.
I mean, he could be Jack the Ripper. Love
to Marta and Pipsqueak.
Ellie xox

✉ From: fingarden@hotmail.com
To: johannavanheerden@hotmail.co.uk

Hi Mum,
I know it's still a long way off but

Marta and I were wondering if you'd
like to come to us for Christmas this
year? Ellie and the Eco-Warrior will
probably be rowing up the Amazon in a
recycled cardboard boat and I'm not
sure what the other two are planning
but it would be nice to have any or all
of you here with us for a change - and
especially you. Ellie says you are
having a break in Galway - hope you're
enjoying yourself and I'll give you a
ring next week.
Love from all three of us,
Finn

✉ From: cosmictraveller@yahoo.co.za
To: ellie3os@hotmail.com

Stop worrying about your mother, darling
- she seems to be having the time of
her life, and if anyone deserves it,
she does. I'm very curious about the
boyfriend though, so I might go and see
her in June. Ireland has such mystery.
And let me know if you do go to Chile:
I have a wonderful friend there. She
used to be a banker too - we met in
Kathmandu. I must say your Carlos is
very handsome - is he an Aries? Look

after yourself, sweetie, and do come and
see me soon.
Big hug and kiss from your favourite
aunt,
Freddy xx

Chapter 10

Achill Island is a place of magic, of sea cliffs and wheeling birds. There are tiny beaches where amethysts wash ashore, and a deserted village on the hillside. Achill lies off the coast of County Mayo, and on this western edge of Ireland the evenings are long and light; and every seven years – or so they say – the magical island of Hy Brasil can be seen on the horizon. We didn't see Hy Brasil but we found a small, family-owned hotel where we ate like kings and where we fell asleep at night under old-fashioned quilts in a room with sloping eaves and with the sound of the Atlantic in our ears. We spent four days there in early May, and when we left the island, and drove back over the causeway to the mainland, a little chip of my heart was left behind forever.

I came back to Belfast to find the garden in full spring bloom and Tiger Lily, who had been staying upstairs with Sticky

Wicket, noticeably fatter. Back at work, nothing much had changed, apart from the addition of some boxes of chipped porcelain, a small painting of a particularly gloomy Madonna and an extra layer of dust.

Archie was waiting for me. He kissed me on both cheeks and then stood back to study me. 'My goodness, Johanna – how well you are looking!'

'Thank you, Archie. I'm sorry I can't say the same for you.' It was true: he looked awful. There were dark rings under his eyes and his normally rosy skin had a distinctly pasty look. 'Have you been ill?'

'It's Morris,' said Archie, in tragic tones. 'I took him to the vet yesterday and they've kept him in for tests: I'm so worried about him that I couldn't sleep a wink.'

'Oh, Archie, I'm sorry! Do they have any idea what might be wrong?'

'Diabetes was mentioned, or it could be hyperthyroidism. I knew there was *something* wrong: he's been so lethargic lately.'

In all the time I'd worked for Archie, I had never seen Morris bestir himself at all, except as dinnertime approached: Lethargy could have been his middle name. However, I kept the thought to myself and patted my employer consolingly on his drooping shoulder. 'Well, we'll just have to keep our fingers crossed, and I'm sure whatever it is, they'll do the best they can for him.'

But Archie, as I told Albert over lunch the following day,

was not to be cheered. 'He's sunk in gloom: he's not eating – which isn't necessarily a bad thing given that he could afford to lose a few pounds – but he's getting under my feet in the shop because he can't concentrate on anything, not even bridge or his latest book.'

'Well, I wouldn't be too worried about his writing,' said Albert. 'It might be a service to literature if he stopped altogether. But obviously he needs distracting. Why don't I come back to the shop with you now and invite him over to give his opinion of my disputed Dufy?'

'You've got a painting by Dufy?' I asked.

'It's very small,' said Albert modestly, 'and almost certainly a fake.'

I felt a strange mixture of emotions: gratitude, primarily, for Albert's eternal readiness to do someone a kindness if he could, and something less pleasant, which must have shown on my face because he took my hand and leant forward anxiously.

'Is that not a good idea, my darling? I just thought it might be something that would interest him …'

'Of course it would,' I replied, 'and it's a kind thought.' I took a deep breath. 'The trouble is, Albert, that I didn't know you had a Dufy because I've only ever been to your house once, and all I saw then was the kitchen. And I don't want Archie having a guided tour when I haven't even had one myself.'

Albert sat back with a look of dismay on his face. Then he nodded. 'You are quite right, Johanna. Phone Archie and ask him if he can do without you for another hour or two and we'll go over to Chestnut Avenue now.'

Twenty minutes later I was standing in Albert's bedroom looking at the Dufy. It was small, but it was charming: a little impressionistic seascape of a cobalt blue bay with palms and toytown houses, and a sailing boat out on the water.

'I don't think it matters who painted it,' I said. 'It's delightful. And if you knew for certain it was worth a fortune, you'd have to worry about it. As it is you can just hang it on the wall and enjoy it. I wonder where it was painted?'

'It could be Nice,' said Albert. 'My father bought it from a dealer in London when he was a young man. He had an eye for things like that – those pots were his as well.'

Above the fireplace stood two blue and white Chinese jars, alongside a brass candlestick and assorted photographs of Norah and Rosie. The fireplace itself was full of books, as were the shelves along the walls. By now I had seen Albert's living room, which was also lined with overflowing bookshelves, his study (ditto) and his two spare bedrooms: there were bookcases everywhere, and where there were no shelves, there were heaps of books and journals stacked against the walls. Anthropology, history, art and philosophy fought for space with literature, politics, film studies and any other subject you might care to name. If ever Good Intentions ran out of stock, I thought, I would know exactly where to come. There was even a pile of books poking out from under his bed.

The bed itself was old-fashioned, brass, and inviting, but I forced myself to concentrate on the painting. 'I suppose we ought to be getting back,' I said, 'but I'm sure Archie would love to see this. Oh Albert, I wish we were there now, walking along the promenade, arm in arm, in sunny Nice – or wherever it is!'

'We will, my darling, and we'll go to Paris too, I promise you, just as soon as all this family business has been sorted out.'

I'd forgotten all about his family, although it occurred to me now that they were almost certainly out at work, which was why the house next door was so silent and Albert had felt it was safe to bring me round.

'I want to walk with you along the Seine, and through the arcades, and take you to all my favourite galleries,' Albert continued. 'You have such an eye for art, Johanna, and such an extraordinary feeling for history.'

I must confess that before meeting Albert I had been unaware of any particular sensitivity towards history, my knowledge of the subject having been confined to the carefully censored version taught at the time in South African schools, and therefore full of holes, but who was I to contradict an expert?

'There is nothing I'd like more,' I said. 'What about August? For my birthday?'

'August isn't a very good month for Paris.' Albert shook his head. 'But September would be perfect – would that do, my darling?'

'Paris in September,' I whispered. 'Oh yes, Albert, that would do very well indeed.'

We got back to the shop to find the closed sign up and a note from Archie to say he had gone to collect Morris from the vet's. I spent an hour polishing a collection of glass bottles and arranging some rather ugly ceramics that Archie had assured me were art deco and well worth the sum he was asking for them. Not a soul came in, apart from Mad Mabel who was convinced that the shop was built directly over a ley line, and had come to check the vibrations. I made a mental note to introduce her to Frederika if I ever got the chance, but otherwise I ignored her. And then, just as I was about to lock up, a taxi drew up outside and Archie emerged with Morris.

'Well?' I demanded anxiously as I held the front door open for them. 'How is he?'

A low yowl informed me that the patient was still alive, but the news was not entirely reassuring. 'It's his heart,' said Archie. 'Apparently it's quite common in older cats, but with the right care and medication, and a bit of luck, he should have a few good years yet.'

'Well, let us hope so,' I said to Albert that weekend. 'I dread to think what Archie will be like if poor old Morris doesn't pull through. And that reminds me, I must remember to take Tiger Lily to the vet next week. She's eating so much, I'm afraid she might have worms. And she'll need to be spayed before she's much older.'

Tiger Lily, who had draped herself adoringly over Albert's knees, suddenly rolled over, offering him her snow-white tummy to be stroked.

'I think it might be a bit late for that,' Albert said, probing gently. 'This cat isn't fat, she's pregnant.'

'She can't be!' I sat bolt upright in surprise. 'She's barely out of kittenhood!'

'Ah well,' said Albert, 'some girls are quicker off the mark than others. I'm pretty sure I'm right though – here, feel for yourself.' And taking my hand he laid it on Tiger Lily's undeniably swollen belly.

'You shameless hussy!' I told her, as she stretched and purred voluptuously. 'What are we going to do now?'

Albert lifted her gently on to my lap and headed for the kitchen. 'We're going to have our coffee,' he said, 'and while I make it, you can think about how you are going to break the news to Sticky Wicket.'

Tiger Lily's kittens were born at the end of May, with remarkably little fuss, in the cupboard in which their mother elected to give birth – ignoring, in the manner of cats, the comfortable basket I had prepared for the event. There were three of them. By the time they had made the transition from blind, rather rat-like newborns to fluffy grey and white copies of their mother, both Albert and Sticky Wicket had lost their hearts entirely. And Archie, shown their pictures, pronounced them quite enchanting.

The same could not be said of Morris. Despite Archie's tender care, his coat had gradually lost its shine, his appetite had dwindled, and he was spending more and more of his time asleep in a basket under the desk. One morning, when I came back with a cup of tea from the minuscule kitchen at the rear of the shop, I noticed that he seemed unnaturally still – and when I prodded him very gently, there was no response. Further prodding only confirmed my fears: Morris had departed.

I felt an unexpected wave of sorrow; I stroked his poor old head softly, and drew his blanket gently over him. Then I felt a rush of panic: Archie was out, but he would be back soon and it would be up to me to break the news. In urgent need of moral support, I rang Albert, who was extremely sympathetic, and unusually practical.

'Put the closed sign up,' he said, 'as a mark of respect and to make sure there's no one around when Archie gets back. Then make yourself another cup of tea, and when he does get back, ask him what we can do to help. He may not have anywhere to bury him.'

So I did all that, and when Archie returned, I broke the news as gently as I could. Then I drew back Morris's blanket and as Archie began to weep, I put my arms around him and wept too. I helped him carry Morris back upstairs and left him to mourn while I went down to the Good Intentions Bookshop, where, as luck would have it, Agnes, the great animal-lover, was on duty.

Archie, who had a horror of graves, had already told me that he could not bear to bury Morris: instead, he wanted him cremated – and Agnes, as I had known she would, could tell me exactly how and where it could be done.

A week or two later, Albert and I drove Archie, clutching a discreet package, up through the north of the city. Our destination was Belfast Castle, a building with a fine outlook over the lough and a formal garden which has greatly appealed to me ever since Albert first took me there, because of its association with cats. There are cats hidden in various places within its walls: mosaic cats, stone ones and others which I shall not describe because I do not want to spoil the surprise for future searchers, but there is one very obvious large stone cat that sits in a bed on the far side of the garden, looking down at its feet with an expression of benign interest. So when Archie finally began to think about where to scatter Morris's ashes, it was the memory of this cat that flashed into my mind and prompted my suggestion.

It was a clear, mild, early summer morning when we descended the stairs into the garden. A couple of tourists were photographing each other beside the fountain, but we strolled as nonchalantly as we could towards our chosen spot, and the moment everyone else disappeared from view and the coast was clear, we sprang into action. Archie stepped forward and very gently and carefully emptied the little bag of ashes into the patch of shrubbery watched over by the stone cat. He murmured something that I didn't catch; then I whispered 'Goodbye. Morris!' and Albert said 'Happy hunting, old fella.' After which we turned to look at each other, and for the first time since Morris's death, Archie smiled.

I have not the slightest idea if what we did was legal – I suspect it was not – but at the time it felt the perfect thing to do. Indeed, Archie's smile turned into a chuckle; then with one accord, like successful criminals, we high-fived before beating a hasty retreat.

Chapter 11

The week after we scattered Morris's ashes was the week of Rosie's birthday, and also the first time since Easter that I had been deprived of Albert's company for more than a couple of days. We had one or two late-night, hurried phone calls, but they were not very satisfactory: Albert's house was crammed with visiting relatives and he was feeling the strain. I missed him badly; I went to work, I did my best to cheer Archie up, and I spent hours playing with Tiger Lily and her kittens, but time dragged nonetheless.

It was during these dog days that I went to visit Agnes – and encountered M. Heaney in the flesh. I also rang my old friend Rita, whom I had neglected of late, and arranged to meet her for lunch on Botanic Avenue. There was a restaurant we wanted to try – a new one seemed to spring up every other week in that area and then close down as quickly as it had opened, and this was to be no exception.

It was called The Courgette and had a vaguely Mediterranean

theme. It also had a very sparse menu, so it didn't take us long to decide what to eat.

'And two large glasses of the house red,' directed Rita, when we had ordered, adding, 'at least that will give us some protection against dysentery. I have my doubts about this place.' Then she leaned forward, folded her arms on the table, and said. 'Right. Tell me *all*.'

Rita is a good listener; she is also a lawyer, and she doesn't beat about the bush. By the time our food arrived – some sort of aubergine quiche with a wilting salad – Rita had marshalled the salient facts and was ticking them off on her fingers: 'You are madly in love: he is kind, honourable, funny, and he makes your knees knock. So far so good. He is separated from his wife but not actually divorced, and he still lives next door to her. Less good. Despite knowing each other (in the biblical as well as the literal sense) for six months, you have only been to his house twice and you have not made any progress in getting to know his family or friends. Also less good. He has promised to put his house on the market so that you and he can find somewhere to set up home together, but for one reason or another he has not yet done so. If I may be frank, Johanna, alarm bells are ringing.'

'I can see why you feel like that,' I said, 'but you need to remember that Albert, for all his other wonderful qualities, is not exactly decisive. Also, he suffers from guilt.'

Rita and I both took thoughtful sips of our wine while we

considered this foreign condition. 'Furthermore,' I continued – consorting with lawyers has this effect on my speech – 'furthermore, he is concerned that Rosie, his youngest daughter, should have as happy a twenty-first birthday as possible: once that's out of the way, it will be full speed ahead.'

'Well, I certainly hope so,' said Rita, 'but long experience inclines me to a pessimistic outlook. I also have a pessimistic outlook concerning the future of this establishment: that quiche was dire. And put your purse away, Johanna – I probably earn more in a week than you do in a year.'

She paid the bill, gave me a rib-crushing hug, and tottered off on her six-inch scarlet heels to her next meeting, while I crossed the road to Good Intentions, where I found Dolores and Sybilla on duty.

'Oh Johanna, how nice to see you,' Dolores said. 'I was just saying to Sybilla that I hoped you'd be in. Agnes has left a note for you, and Mrs Chung brought in one of her cakes this morning, so if you'll hold the fort with Sybilla, I'll go and put the kettle on for tea.'

A small flurry of customers distracted us for the next few minutes; then a woman staggered in with several bin bags of books, which I offered to unpack. They contained a fairly standard mixture of dog-eared paperbacks, old library books, out-of-date text books, chipped ornaments, some *Reader's Digest* magazines and a grubby vest.

By the time I got round to opening Agnes's note, Dolores

had returned with the tea and Mrs Chung's cake. Mrs Chung was a great favourite in the bookshop: tiny and smiling, she had come from Hong Kong with her husband some twenty years earlier, and had thrown herself heart and soul into life in Belfast. Whether she could make Peking duck or dim sum I have no idea, but her soda and potato breads were famous, and her cakes were fabulous. She came into the bookshop every week to stock up on reading matter (she favoured crime novels of the more gruesome sort) and every so often she brought the staff a cake. This week's offering was chocolate, and as the quiche across the road had been less than satisfying, I helped myself to a large slice.

As for Agnes, the note was typical of her kindness: she was just writing to say that she hoped that all had gone according to plan with the scattering of Morris's ashes and that she sent her best wishes to Archie and hoped he was bearing up.

'Did Agnes tell you about Archie's cat?' I asked Sybilla and Dolores.

'She told us she'd helped you arrange his cremation,' Sybilla replied. 'Did it all work out?'

'Better than we could have hoped,' I said, and I described for them the clandestine scattering of the ashes in the castle gardens.

They roared with laughter, which caused one of the more foolhardy customers to remark that it was as well for some, sitting there eating chocolate cake with their feet up and not even offering a regular customer so much as a bite.

'The last thing you need is a slice of cake, Big Eddie,' said Dolores, eyeing him unkindly. 'Away off and bother them at Oxfam, why don't you?' She turned back to the cake and held the knife poised. 'Another piece, Johanna?'

'Thank you, no. But I was just thinking, perhaps I could take a slice up to Archie? He's in the shop this afternoon and I'm sure he'd appreciate it. Anyway, I want to show him Agnes's note.'

I found Archie sitting behind the desk, staring mournfully into space. There was no one in the shop.

'Archie,' I said, 'I've brought you some of Mrs Chung's chocolate cake, and a kind note from Agnes. I'll just go and put the kettle on and then I want to talk to you about an idea I've had.'

My idea was very simple: it was that Archie should take a little holiday. I knew that his devotion to Morris and his distrust of catteries had prevented him from going away for years. Now was the perfect moment for him to have a change of scene. In another month it might be different, but I reckoned it would take at least that long before he might be ready to consider another feline companion. I had one of Tiger Lily's kittens in mind as a replacement, of course, but for the time being, I kept that plan to myself.

Archie, as I expected, was initially resistant.

'My sister?' he said, in answer to my first suggestion. 'We

haven't seen each other for twenty years, an arrangement that is entirely satisfactory to us both. And I have no wish to go to Australia.'

'Europe, then. Think of the art, the antiques, the culture!'

'I don't care for flying,' said Archie.

'You and Albert both. Very well then, what about Scotland? You could take the ferry.'

'Unfortunately not: I am a martyr to seasickness.'

'Well, that leaves Ireland, which is after all the obvious choice. There is no reason at all why you shouldn't take your car and make a leisurely progress from one charming county to the next. You *like* driving – and think of all those delightful little hotels you could stay in, like the one we stayed in on Achill Island.' It was time to play my trump card. 'Archie, think of the food!'

I had already described in detail the wild Atlantic salmon, the melting lamb and the glorious homemade bread that Albert and I had enjoyed.

'And who would look after the shop?'

'I would, of course. I can easily do a few extra days. You could be away tomorrow, Archie, and I would promise to take great care of everything. Take ten days – take two weeks! It will do you all the good in the world.'

It would also, I reflected, do me good. Albert's Rosie would be celebrating her birthday that weekend and the family celebrations were set to continue throughout the following week.

I had nothing planned, and no chance of seeing my beloved, so getting Archie organised and taking over the running of the shop would be as good a project as any to keep me busy.

And so I was left in charge of Archibald's Antiques for what turned out to be a period of ten days. In the beginning Archie telephoned me at least once a day, but by the middle of the first week he had begun to adjust, and after that when the phone in the shop rang, it was usually Albert, who had been press-ganged into chauffeuring the visiting relatives to the various far-flung farms and villages where their multitudinous cousins dwelt. He would ring and say that if he never saw another slice of fruit soda or drank another cup of dark brown tea, it would be too soon. This was some comfort to me, but not a lot.

In the meantime, customers came and went (occasionally) and Archie's Friday and Saturday cronies took the shock of finding me in his place with the quiet resignation so common to men who spend their lives pursuing postage stamps and postcards.

It would have been a fairly dreary week, had it not been for a phone call I received on the Friday night. It was my sister Frederika.

'Hanna? Good, I was hoping you'd be in. What are you up to this weekend?'

'Not much. I'm looking after the shop tomorrow but Albert's still tied up with his family.'

'In that case you can pick me up from the airport on Sunday,' said Frederika. 'I've booked a flight out tomorrow. I get in to Heathrow at the crack of dawn on Sunday and I'll be in Belfast in time for lunch. I've got to rush out now but I'll email you the details. Can't wait to see you, sweetie!' And the line went dead.

'Well I never!' I said to Tiger Lily, who was gazing down at me from the top of a cupboard. She had gone from being a proud and attentive mother to being rather bored with the whole affair and frequently scaled great heights to avoid her offspring. 'The planets must be in favourable alignment!' And I went off, humming happily, to clear the spare bedroom for my sister.

Chapter 12

In all the years I have lived in Northern Ireland, I do not think I have ever had a visitor on whom the rain did not fall for at least some – and frequently all – of their stay. Frederika was the exception. She flew in to glorious sunshine and the weather held until she left.

At first I cursed the fact that I had sent Archie off on holiday and committed myself to the shop, but in the end it turned out very well: Freddy was entirely happy to explore the city on her own, returning periodically to Archibald's Antiques to catch her breath and dump her purchases, and once introduced to the Good Intentions Bookshop, she could only be prised out with difficulty.

On the Wednesday afternoon Archie rang to say he would be back the following day, so it was in happy anticipation of the rest of the week off that I closed the shop and went in search of my sister. I found her, as expected, in the bookshop, where she was deep in conversation with a long-haired young man who sported a checked keffiyeh and an array of badges proclaiming him to be in favour of anarchists, whales, Jesus, Greenpeace and Palestine, and against capitalism, fracking and homophobia.

'Hello, Dylan,' I said. 'I see you've met my sister. When did you get back?'

'Last week,' he replied. 'And oh boy, Johanna, is it ever good to be back here! One more day in the States and I would have gone crazy.'

'Poor Dylan has an arch-conservative family in deepest Missouri,' I explained to Frederika. 'He goes home once a year hoping for a bit of truth and reconciliation but is always disappointed. Still, at least this time you seem to have come back unscathed!' This was perhaps unkind, being a reference to a previous occasion when Dylan had returned sporting a black eye.

'And what are you doing here in Belfast?' my sister enquired.

'I teach a course in conflict resolution,' Dylan told her, 'but, like Johanna, I help out in the bookshop when I can.'

'Well, good for you!' said Frederika. 'Of course, as a South African, the whole subject of conflict resolution is of enormous interest to me, but to get back to what we were discussing a moment ago, what Deepak Chopra really meant was …'

I decided that this was as good a moment as any to excuse myself; besides, I could see Dolores signalling to me with her eyebrows, so I went over to the counter.

'He's found a soulmate in your sister,' she said. 'Apparently they are both into Guerilla Gardening and Cosmic Ordering – or maybe it was Cosmic Gardening and Guerilla Ordering. Whatever – they're as mad as each other. I like her, mind you, and she's bought a whole clatter of books.'

A pile of books to one side of the counter bore witness to this: Frederika appeared to have cleaned out the section loosely known as Loony Fringe.

'She used to be a top investment banker,' I told Dolores, 'until she went to India and found Enlightenment. Fortunately she made an awful lot of money first.'

The enlightened one chose that moment to break off her conversation with Dylan and announce to the room at large that she was going to take us all out for a drink. 'At The Craic,' she said. 'Is that right? Dylan tells me that no holiday in Belfast is complete without a visit to The Craic.'

'Are you mad?' I asked? 'This *is* The Craic we're talking about? As in "lively conversation" – only in this case the full name is The Craic of Doom. It's a den of thieves! We'd be lucky to get out of there with our lives!'

Dolores backed me up – she said visits were terminated rather than completed in The Craic – but our words were in vain: Frederika was determined to have her way. Despite a half-hearted protest about there still being ten minutes to closing time, we were chivvied into locking up and then bundled into a taxi in short order. A second taxi followed, containing the three or four customers who had been in the shop at the time, and had therefore included themselves in Freddy's invitation.

As expected, the pub turned out to be one of Belfast's murkier establishments, but my sister was in her element, and even without the vast amounts of alcohol she insisted on paying for, it wouldn't have taken long for everyone to fall under her spell. The thing about Frederika is that she is a brilliant storyteller and she has an endless fund of (ever more colourful) anecdotes about our childhood in Gauteng. By the time she had described the occasion when our brothers, Kobus, Stefanus and Jannie, had tried to charm a cobra, and had regaled the growing audience with the scandalous affair of our aunt Katrien and the policeman, she had them hanging on her every word.

The other thing about Freddy is that once she gets into her stride, she's not easy to stop. So one drink turned into two, and two to three, and it was only when Dolores turned to me and said, 'She's good craic, your sister, I'll say that for her, but it's high time I was away,' that I realised just how long we had been there. I also realised that I had had very little to eat, and far too much to drink, and that it was going to take some ingenuity to dislodge Frederika. So I excused myself, along with Dolores, and staggered out into the night air to ring Albert.

'Thank God,' I said when he answered. 'Are you home?'

'I'm just in this minute,' he replied. 'Where are you?'

I told him.

'Good grief!' said Albert. 'What are you doing *there*?'

'Drinking with my sister,' I said. 'You wouldn't like to come and take us away, would you?'

Albert was impressively decisive. 'I'll be there in five minutes,' he said, and rang off.

Fortunately, Frederika's curiosity is powerful, and she was dying to meet Albert. Of course she wanted him to come in and join us but I told her no, he was driving, and that no one ever drank and drove in this part of the world, whatever they still did in the less civilised reaches of Gauteng. It also helped that the pub was becoming noticeably noisier and more crowded, and that the earlier raffish but good-humoured atmosphere was beginning to deteriorate – proving, not for the first time, that Dolores had a finely-honed instinct for getting out when the going was good. It was obvious to me too that Dylan's conflict resolution skills might soon be called upon, and I had less faith in them leading to peace and harmony than to total mayhem.

So in the end I got my sister out of there without too much difficulty, and Albert, to my great relief, was waiting with the engine running – no doubt to facilitate a quick getaway, should one be needed. I pushed Freddy into the passenger seat and climbed into the back, intending to lie down, but the moment I put my head down, it spun in a way I had not experienced since my student days, so I propped myself back up and listened to Freddy and Albert getting acquainted.

My sister had drunk at least as much as I had, but as her head has always been a great deal harder than mine, she showed no sign of it. Instead she bombarded Albert with questions, and he responded. By the time we got home, they were mutually charmed, and a plan had been hatched for Albert to collect us the following morning to drive us down to the Mournes.

There are many routes into the heart of the Mourne Mountains, but for me the simplest (and least strenuous) is to start from the Carrick Little car park above the village of Annalong, where a gently climbing track crosses the dry-stone boundary that is the Mourne Wall and leads you north into the mountains. In no time at all you find that you have left the world behind you and have entered the domain of wind and sheep and scudding clouds, where the peaks of Slieve Binnian, Slieve Donard and Slieve Lamagan surround you and the only sounds are those of the birds and the little stream that tumbles downhill.

Frederika was enchanted. As we paused for breath at a bend in the track – Albert, who is extremely fit, was striding on ahead – she turned to me and said, 'I can see why you love it here. And I can see why you love Albert – he's very attractive, and he really *listens*, which is so unusual in a man. I'm not surprised though: I was struck at once by his aura – it has a most unusual glow.'

'Really? And what about mine?'

'Oh, you're very pink at the moment,' said Freddy, and gave me a sphinx-like smile.

Our destination that day was the Blue Lough, which for once lived up to its name, reflecting the brilliant sky above us. There is always a wind up there but the clouds that flew overhead were white and fluffy, and the sun shone brightly on the three of us as we perched on a group of boulders and shared a bottle of ice-cold mountain water that Albert had filled on the way up.

From the Blue Lough a short walk will take you up to another ridge, and more panoramic views, but we decided to turn back, because Freddy and I were both famished, and Albert had promised us lunch in Warrenpoint, which was still a fair way off. Accordingly, we set off down the track, scrambling over boulders and continuing down through open heathland, and along the side of Annalong wood, until we came in view of the sea once more. We passed the odd hiker going north, and one or two runners, but it was only when we were climbing over the stone stile that crossed the wall that Freddy said, 'We seem to have lost our companion.'

'What companion?' asked Albert.

'That woman who has been behind us most of the way.'

'I didn't see anyone,' I said. 'What did she look like?'

'I couldn't see her face,' Freddy replied, 'but it was definitely a woman. She was wearing a blue dress – I remember wondering if she was cold without a jacket.'

Albert had come to a dead halt.

'Good heavens,' he said. 'I wonder if it was the Blue Lady.'

'Who's the Blue Lady?' we asked in unison.

'The ghost of a woman who was abandoned by her husband – local legend has it that she haunts these parts.' Albert was looking at Frederika with a combination of awe and alarm; I, on the other hand, regarded her with some suspicion. My sister is, after all, a woman who loves a good story above all things, and it seemed to me entirely possible that she had come upon the legend in her guide book and had seized the chance to lay the foundations of yet another gripping yarn – a suspicion that was in no way dispelled when she turned and gave me the very faintest shadow of a wink.

Our expedition to the Blue Lough was followed two days later by one to the north coast, specifically to see the Giant's Causeway. I am with Dr Johnson on this one: it is worth seeing, but not worth going to see, being a long way from Belfast even on the most direct and least interesting route. And if you take the Coastal Route, it is a much longer drive altogether, and the chances are that you will be so intoxicated by the scenery along the way that you will be in no hurry at all to get to the causeway itself. But Albert was happy to act as our chauffeur – which was good of him, considering how much driving he had done lately – and we had a very pleasant day out.

With just one day left before she was due to fly home, Freddy declared that we should have a farewell lunch with the three men in my life. And so she invited Albert, Sticky Wicket and Archie – whom she had never met, but who was inveigled into coming by the promise of a gourmet South African meal. It was also decided that he would share a taxi with Albert because there was to be no stinting on food or drink, and no one was to be allowed to drive. Freddy let me peel and chop and lay the table, but otherwise she insisted I leave her to it: in cooking, as in storytelling, I bow to my sister's superior talents. And Frederika in charge is a force to behold, and a reminder of just why she was so successful in her earlier career. It is also something to be grateful for that her later 'enlightenment' did not extend to vegetarianism, because her lamb bredie – lamb, golden onions, ripe tomatoes and long thin green beans – and her sweet potatoes and spicy chicken are the food of heaven. By the time the guests had assembled, the flat was full of mouth-watering smells and the table held such an artistic presentation of dishes that it seemed a shame to disturb them. We did though, and we also drank a great deal of excellent South African wine as we demolished Freddy's feast.

'Superb!' said Archie, leaning back – to the peril of his chair – and patting his lips with his napkin. He wasn't finished, he was merely taking a short break. 'My dear Frederika, I congratulate you.'

'Absolutely top-notch!' Sticky Wicket agreed. 'Can't think when I had a meal like it.'

And Albert, raising his glass to us, toasted the 'Sensational van Heerden Sisters', which was very gallant, as well as being an impressive piece of articulation considering how much wine he had drunk. There was cheese and fruit to follow, and then, just as I had steered Archie over to the largest armchair in the room,

Tiger Lily, with unerring timing, brought in her kittens for inspection.

'Oh dear me!' Archie bent down to scoop one on to his lap. 'How irresistible they are! What have you called them, Johanna?'

'Nothing as yet,' I answered, 'because I can't possibly keep them, much as I'd like to, and if I give them names I'll get too attached to let them go.'

The kitten on Archie's lap danced up the gentle slope of his stomach and burrowed into his neck just as her sister began to ascend his left leg. He was weakening before my eyes.

'Anyway, it really is high time I found homes for them. I suppose I could try Cats' Protection ...'

'All right, dammit,' said Archie, 'I'll take one.'

'Why not have two?' Frederika suggested. 'They'd be company for each other. And Sticky Wicket could have the other. That way Tiger Lily would still have one of her kittens in this house, they'd all have good homes, and everyone would be happy.'

And so it was that Albert and Archie departed in a taxi with two kittens in a basket while Sticky Wicket meekly and carefully bore the third upstairs. As for Tiger Lily, she gave what appeared to me to be a heartfelt sigh of relief as she curled herself up in undisturbed possession of her favourite armchair once again.

The following morning my sister flew out. The sun which had shone so steadily throughout her stay vanished with her plane; the rain fell in torrents, and not even the prospect of having Albert all to myself for the first time in weeks could stop my tears from falling too.

Chapter 13

The rain fell for most of July. It didn't stop the time-honoured practice of enthusiastic marching and drum-banging, with the occasional riot thrown in, for several days on either side of the Twelfth – the date which commemorates the Battle of the Boyne, when William of Orange defeated King James II. As this event took place in 1690 you would think that all parties would have had enough time to get over it, but apparently not.

Archie shut up shop for the week, to avoid having his windows broken by over-excited members of the populace and to devote himself to getting to know his kittens, whom he had named Jasmine and Rose. Sticky Wicket had called his Fred, in honour of my sister. Meanwhile, Albert and I took ourselves off to remote corners where we were least likely to run into marching bands.

It was on one of these excursions that we finally conquered Slieve Croob. I had studied the map with care, and by taking the Dromara Road from Ballynahinch, through Massford to Finnis, we found the way at last to the car park on the slopes of the peak.

It was a wild and windswept place, but an easy enough walk, and by following the track right round the front of the communications towers that crown the summit, we found ourselves looking out at a breathtaking panorama of the Mournes. We stood there, arm in arm, watching the light play on their velvet slopes and on the distant sea.

'According to M. Heaney, Slieve Croob used to be a Lughnasa assembly site, where people came to celebrate a sort of harvest festival dedicated to the sun god, Lugh,' I informed Albert, as we retraced our steps to the car park.

'An invaluable source of information, Mr Heaney,' said Albert. 'I'm looking forward to his next book.'

I had told Albert about my unexpected meeting with the author on the day of my visit to Agnes and the Giant's Ring, and I was looking forward to the *Guide to Ancient County Antrim* as well – not least because we had by now pretty much exhausted ancient County Down and I was planning to extend our travels into other counties, not to mention other countries.

It was with this in mind that I broached the subject of my birthday some days later.

We had driven down to Seapark, where we left the car, one sunny Monday morning, and were about halfway along the coastal path from Holywood to Bangor. This is a favourite walk of mine, and there is a particular bench, hidden from the path by a bank of shrubbery, which has a lovely view of the bay and is a good place to stop. It is also an excellent spot for undisturbed conversation. Or so I thought.

At any rate, it began well: Albert's arm was around me, my head on his shoulder, the air full of birdsong and the gentle lap of water in the cove below us. I sighed with pleasure, and marshalled my thoughts. Uppermost in my mind was the sale of Albert's house: in my more optimistic moments I imagined it going through in time for us to have moved into our own home by Christmas, but with everything on hold over July, I had reluctantly decided that it was a little soon to expect any major developments. Besides, I had more immediate matters to raise.

'Albert,' I said, 'we need to decide on a date for our trip to Paris.'

'Oh there's still plenty of time,' he replied.

'But hotels and flights get booked up so quickly at this time of year. I don't mind going online to see what's available' – Albert, despite being perfectly able to use his computer, still tended to regard it as an instrument of the devil – 'but I do need to have some idea of when it suits us both to go.' I took a deep breath. 'And I also need to book my flight home to South Africa.'

'Well, why don't we think about going to Paris at the end of September?' Albert suggested. 'Or we might even wait until

October: autumn in Paris is a beautiful time.'

I straightened up and spoke firmly. 'No, Albert, October will not do. I have set my heart on September. Of course, if you've changed your mind …'

'Johanna, my darling, of course I haven't!' Albert took both my hands and raised them to his lips. 'South Africa might have to wait a little longer, but there is nothing I want more than to take you to Paris. It's just that there are a few domestic matters that might tie me up for the first half of the month.'

'What sort of domestic matters?'

'There's a lot of urgent work that has to be done on the house,' Albert said. 'Painting and plastering, and the loft needs to be insulated. It will take a couple of weeks at least, and the man who usually helps me out rang yesterday to say he's not free until September …'

I softened temporarily: after all, he probably hoped that all these improvements would help to secure a better price. Besides, it always touched me that Albert took so much pride in DIY – and was surprisingly good at it. It had formed another unexpected bond between him and Sticky Wicket. But even as I looked at him fondly, I had a sudden and distinct memory of an earlier conversation between them on the very subject of loft insulation – a subject Albert had been well up on. And the reason for his being so well informed, I now recalled, was that he had only recently insulated his own loft. I withdrew my hands and fixed him with a steely eye.

'It is your house that we're talking about?'

Albert looked at his shoes.

'I see. You want to postpone our trip to Paris, my birthday trip to Paris, because you have undertaken to do some work, not on your house – the one that is supposed to be up for sale so that you and I can move into a new one together – but on your estranged wife's house. Carmel's house. Have I got that right?'

I'm not sure what Albert would have said in response because it was at that moment that we became aware of voices on the path above us, and a moment later two people stepped around the bank of shrubbery and halted in their tracks when they saw us sitting on the bench.

'Good heavens!' Albert gave a feeble laugh. 'Norah and Kevin!'

I had only seen Norah on that one occasion at Chestnut Avenue and I hadn't realised how pretty she was. Either that or her looks had improved: her dark hair shone and her cheeks had that rose-petal blush that is one of the few benefits of living in a sunless climate. She was in better humour too because she greeted me quite cordially before embracing her father and sitting down beside him.

'What are you doing here?' she asked.

'Walking to Bangor,' Albert replied. 'Are you doing the same?'

'We're going in the opposite direction,' said Norah. 'It was such a nice morning we decided to take a day off and clear our heads.'

'Had a bit of a party last night,' confided Kevin. I don't think I'd heard him speak before – his voice was unexpectedly attractive, with a soft country accent. Then he leaned towards me and hissed, 'Did you see the ring?'

Norah giggled and held out her left hand in the sunlight. On the fourth finger a diamond sparkled.

'You're engaged?' I felt a rush of happiness for them – I've always been a pushover for romance. 'Congratulations! When did this happen?'

'Didn't Daddy tell you? It was just after Rosie's birthday. We couldn't let her hog all the limelight!'

'Well, I'm delighted for you both. And have you set a date for the wedding?'

'December,' said Norah.

'December? This year?'

'Yes. We've got Christmas jobs in a ski resort in Scotland, so we'll be having a working honeymoon.'

I knew that Norah was a physiotherapist, that Kevin had some sort of job in IT, and that they had been saving hard to buy a house of their own. I also knew they shared a passion for the more vigorous type of outdoor activity – in particular, winter sports – so I was genuinely pleased for them that they had been able to make such a sensible and satisfactory arrangement.

Then Norah laughed and patted her father's knee. 'Poor Daddy, though – he's going to have his house full of relatives again, and most of them will probably stay on for Christmas!'

They left soon after that to continue their walk, while we sat on in a lengthening silence.

'Johanna?' After several minutes Albert reached for my hand, but I folded my arms. 'I should have told you before this. I'm sorry.'

'Yes,' I said, 'you should have.'

'Look, I know it means I can't put the house on the market just yet, but spring is probably a better time altogether. And I'm sorry I didn't tell you but I was waiting for the right moment. And what can I do, sweetheart? It's Norah's wedding, after all.'

'I suppose that's why you're all tied up in September? Getting everything shipshape for the celebrations?'

'Johanna, don't be like that! And it's not just the house, there's another problem: Carmel has to go into hospital, and I more or less promised I'd be around in case of emergency.'

'Is it something serious?' I tried not to sound too hopeful.

'She's having her gall bladder removed.'

'Well, you never know, it might improve her disposition. Major surgery or keyhole?'

'Keyhole. But she's very nervous.'

'She'll be out in a day,' I said. 'I was. And does she not have sisters, friends – never mind daughters – who can' hold her hand?'

'Of course she does, but I feel an obligation, Johanna. After all, we've been married for so many years.'

'Indeed,' I replied, 'so many unhappy years – for the last five of which you have been separated. And what about me, Albert? Do you think it's fair to keep stringing me along? To make all these promises, and then disappoint me?' I had started to cry now, the tears trickling down my face. 'I told my friend Rita that you were an honourable man, but I see that I was wrong. You are a dishonourable man, Albert Morrow, and I don't believe that you were ever going to take me to Paris, or sell your house at all!'

There was more. Trust was mentioned, so was love; I regret to say that I may even have spoken of a broken heart – once started, I found it hard to stop. Albert himself said very little, possibly for lack of opportunity, and in the end I was silenced by my tears. So I gathered such pathetic tatters of my dignity as remained and started back the way we had come.

Of course, I realised almost at once that to have embarked on a passionate argument when on foot and far from home had been singularly ill-advised, especially when the object of my fury had no alternative but to take the same path back – and that both of us were bound to be continually accosted by cheerful fools intent on wishing us a good day. Fortunately, I had a pair of sunglasses with me – at least they hid my eyes – but we must still have made a sorry sight, as I stumbled back along the path with Albert trailing after me like a disconsolate shadow.

Chapter 14

✉ From: johannavanheerden@hotmail.com
To: cosmictraveller@yahoo.co.za

Dear Freddy,
Thank you for listening to me sob.
I feel a bit calmer this evening but I
haven't heard a word from Albert for
days. Oh Freddy, what am I going to do?
I want to hear his voice so badly
I can't think of anything else. Part
of me wants to pick up the phone and make
it up, part of me is furious that he
could leave me suffering like this, and
part of me wants to think it's just
a storm in a teacup. I suppose all
I can do is wait for the storm to pass.
J

✉ From: cosmictraveller@yahoo.co.za
   To: johannavanheerden@hotmail.com

Life isn't about waiting for the storm to
pass, darling – it's about learning to
dance in the rain. Be strong! He'll ring.
Speak to you later xxx

✉ From: johannavanheerden@hotmail.com
   To: cosmictraveller@yahoo.co.za

Well, he rang. After leaving me in
despair for days. He said that he hadn't
been well, that the stress of being torn
two ways is unbearable and that perhaps
what we need to do is take a little break
from each other. He said perhaps it
isn't possible to sustain a relationship
of such intensity – he talked about
breathing spaces and emotional demands.
And so on and so forth. I talked about
honesty, broken promises and commitment.
I said we were both too old for this
sort of nonsense, and if he didn't love
me enough to make up his mind, there was
nothing more to be said. Then I put
the phone down.
Sticky Wicket is off for the weekend
watching cricket somewhere so I am cat-
sitting but I am crying so much that

Tiger Lily and Fred are both avoiding me
because I am making them damp. Ring me
when you can.
Johanna

✉ From: cosmictraveller@yahoo.co.za
To: johannavanheerden@hotmail.com

Well Snoekie, it looks as though I was
wrong about Albert's aura. I think what
you need right now is a complete change
of direction: you need to throw yourself
heart and soul into some new project.
What about an art class, or creative
writing, or something like that? I wish I
was there right now to help you through
this - and I haven't forgotten it's your
birthday on the fourteenth. Do you want
me to fly back? Or do you want to come
here? Just say the word if there is
anything at all that I can do - and ring
me any hour of the day or night.
BIG hug and kiss,
Freddy

✉ From: johannavanheerden@hotmail.com
To: cosmictraveller@yahoo.co.za

Dear Freddy,
I don't know what I would have done

without you this last week, and thanks
for the offer to fly back, but it looks as
though I'm going to have company on my
birthday after all. Just when I thought
things couldn't get any worse, Ellie
rang. You're not going to believe this,
Freddy, but her heart is broken too!!
Carlos has decided that he 'needs his
space' - is this an epidemic? - so the
move to Brazil is off and she's coming
home instead. I'm so sad for her, but
also so comforted to think I'm going to
see her again in a few days time - at
least we can be miserable together! And
I'm going to take us out for a slap-up
birthday dinner, and to hell with the
expense! Sticky Wicket and Archie are
both being very sweet to me too, which
helps.
Lots of love,
Johanna x

PS Please thank Thandi and Louise and
tell them that the idea of a curse is
very tempting but on the whole, better
not. I'm afraid I still love him too much
to want him seriously hurt. But they can
put one on Carlos if they want.

✉ From: ellie3os@hotmail.com
To: cosmictraveller@yahoo.co.za

Dear Auntie Fruitloop,
Thank you for your lovely message. Yes I
am very sad, but my attitude is, if he
wants his space, then he's welcome to it
– just as long as he doesn't expect me
to be waiting around when he gets back!
But poor Ma – if I ever meet that weasel
Albert I will tear him limb from limb!
It's lovely to be home though and we
are doing our best to cheer each other
up. I've been going in to work with her
(I adore Archie!) and into the Good
Intentions Bookshop that you liked so
much, and tomorrow night we're going
out to celebrate her birthday with
her friend Rita, which will either
kill us or cure us!
Perhaps you should ask the Kalk Bay Moon
Circle to do a protection spell to keep
us safe?
I wish you were here too – I'm so sorry
I just missed you but I hope to come and
visit you soon.
Lots of love from your favourite niece,
Ellie xxx

✉ From: johannavanheerden@hotmail.com
To: cosmictraveller@yahoo.co.za

Oh God, Freddy, what a night! We started
off in a cocktail bar, then we had an
amazing dinner in Chez Patrice – that
place is so expensive I wouldn't normally
dare step over the threshold but Rita
insisted on paying for everything – and
then we went on to some club where I
danced away the night with boys who were
probably the same age as Finn and Seamus.
I'm afraid I may have made an exhibition
of myself – but I don't care: it was
wonderful! And Ellie enjoyed herself
too. My ears are still ringing and I am
a little hungover but I don't regret a
minute of it.
Love,
Johanna xx

✉ From: johannavanheerden@hotmail.com
To: cosmictraveller@yahoo.co.za

Darling generous Freddy,
Your birthday present just arrived – what
a brilliant idea! I don't think I've
ever seen such an enormous hamper – just
unpacking it was enough to make us swoon!
A thousand thanks from Ellie and me – we

will be gorging on luxuries for days to
come. Although I'm a bit ashamed that
we are both so cheered by food! Did I
tell you that Archie presented me with
a beautiful little antique brooch, and
Sticky Wicket gave me a big bunch of
flowers? But not a single word from Albert
... oh well, I'm going to try to take a
leaf out of Ellie's book and tell myself
that if he doesn't think I am the most
wonderful woman on the planet, then he
doesn't deserve me!
Love,
Johanna xxx

PS I think I might see if I can find a
couple of cheap flights and take Ellie
over to visit Finn and Marta for a couple
of days. I haven't seen them for ages and
it might take our minds off our broken
hearts – once the contents of the hamper
have run out!

Chapter 15

On a sunny day at the end of August, Ellie and I flew to London. I gave her the window seat because I didn't want to look out over Strangford Lough and find myself wondering if one of the little glinting dots moving along the ribbon of road was Albert's car, and who, if anyone, might be with him. I hadn't heard from him since the telephone conversation before my birthday and I hadn't rung him back, or emailed, even though I had been sorely tempted. However, there is one thing to be said for the end of a love affair: you feel so bad that nothing else matters. I found that all the normal irritations and concerns about air travel suddenly dwindled into insignificance; after all, what are queues and searches, restrictions and security alerts – never mind alarming engine noises and the prospect of imminent death – in the face of the all-consuming misery of heartbreak?

As for Ellie, it wrung my heart even more to see her as thin and drawn as she was then. She is my middle child, sandwiched between Finn and the twins, and until now had dealt with life's misfortunes with an unflappable serenity, but on that journey – despite our best efforts – we were both sunk in gloom. Still, there is nothing like a change of scene to lift the spirits, and the sight of Finn waiting to meet us was the best of all possible antidotes to our sad condition.

A year or two earlier, Finn and Marta had started a market-garden business in one of those surprising green patches in the city. Pippa (otherwise known as Pipsqueak) is Marta's six year-old daughter from a previous liaison and is a delightful child whom we all love dearly. The three of them live with several other like-minded souls in a rambling communal house known to Nuala and Seamus as the Organic Ashram.

As Ellie and I followed Finn down the hall, picking our way between bicycles, gumboots, and assorted piles of recycling, a door opened and a small vision in violet dungarees and a floppy hat stitched with sunflowers came flying towards us.

'Granny Finn! Ellie!' Pippa flung her arms around us. 'Mummy's in the garden but first you have to come upstairs and see your room!' She pulled us along behind Finn, who was climbing the stairs with our bags, and danced ahead into a tiny room with a sloping ceiling. Two narrow beds stood on either side of a rag rug, with just enough space for a slightly rickety chair between them; there was an ancient chest of drawers, a jam jar full of daisies, and a tie-dyed curtain looped back from the window with a bootlace. There was also relatively little dust, and, pinned to the wall, a large banner reading WeLcum!

Pippa surveyed her handiwork with satisfaction. 'Doesn't it look nice?' she said. 'I did it nearly all myself. I even did sweeping.'

Ellie picked her up and hugged her. 'It's gorgeous!' she said. 'Better than staying at the Ritz! And I love your outfit – did Mummy make it?'

Pippa nodded, beaming, and Finn said 'Marta's been branching out into children's clothes: she's selling as many as she can make. But she can tell you all about it herself. Come on down now – I'm starving.'

At the back of the house there was a lovely overgrown patch of lawn with apple trees and a hammock, and there we found Marta, setting out a picnic supper.

'We thought we'd eat out here, just the five of us,' she said, after hugs and kisses had been exchanged. 'It's such a lovely evening, and anyway Raj and Sophie won't be back until much later, and Leila has gone to visit her mother. There's so much to catch up on, we don't want to share you with anyone else.'

This was something of a relief to me: meals in that house were strictly communal, and as cooking was done according to a weekly rota, the standard was variable but tended towards lentil stews and vegetable casseroles made from whatever produce remained unsold. A previous visit had coincided with a glut of turnips and I had made a mental note to stay away in winter.

But on this occasion we feasted on summer vegetables and Raj's mother's celebrated samosas, along with homemade dips and elderberry wine – and in my case, mercifully non-organic gin and tonic. Sitting there in the long, summer dusk, we caught up with all the news: Pippa had a great deal to tell us about her first year at school, Ellie and I touched lightly on our very different travels, and Finn and Marta were happy to report a modest growth in the gardening business, as well as an unexpected demand for the children's clothing which Marta had begun as a sideline, but which now threatened to expand into something a lot more time-consuming.

'But profitable,' said Finn, with his characteristic crooked grin, and I thought how well and happy he was looking. He has his father's dark looks but is slighter, and inclined to push himself too hard; now though, he looked utterly contented and relaxed. As for Marta, I had never seen her looking better. Her normally wraith-like presence seemed suddenly rosy, and unusually substantial – and when she stretched up an arm, I thought I saw the reason why.

'Marta! Am I imagining it or are you …' I let my eyes rest on her stomach, and she blushed, and then both she and Finn began to laugh.

'We were saving the best news until last: Pip is going to have a little brother or sister in the New Year. Are you pleased?'

'Pleased? I couldn't be more pleased!' I jumped up and hugged her, and then my son. 'What wonderful news! We should be drinking champagne!'

'We will,' said Ellie. She had thrown her arms around Finn in delight and was now sitting beside Marta, stroking her long pale hair. 'Oh, Marta, what brilliant news. I'm going to be its very favourite aunt.'

'In that case you'll have to stick around,' said Finn. 'You can't be a favourite aunt if you're always off to Ulan Bator or Patagonia.'

'Oh yes I can,' said Ellie. 'I can send back exotic presents and turn up once a year on a camel. I might stay a bit closer to home though – I've been thinking of Spain as it happens. At any rate, I've had enough of South America for the time being.'

There was a little silence, then Marta said softly, 'I'm really sorry, Ellie: Carlos is a moron. But it's nice for us to have you back.'

'Why don't you come back to London for a while?' Finn suggested. 'You can have the room you're staying in now for as long as you like, and you're bound to get work: supply teachers and tutors are always in demand.'

'Or you could help out here,' said Marta. 'We always need a hand.'

'Oh please come!' Pippa beseeched her. 'I want you to live here more than anything in the world!'

'In that case,' said Ellie, 'how can I refuse?'

Soon after we returned to Belfast, Ellie went back to London and I found myself once again on my own. September was a cold, wet month, and the stormy grey waters of the lough were a sad reflection of my mood. I missed my children terribly, but I was delighted that Ellie was putting her life back together again. Tiger Lily, who had obviously been well looked after in my absence, had seemed surprisingly pleased – for a cat – to have me home again, and Fred was often to be found curled up with her on my sofa. Sticky Wicket had indulged in an orgy of cat-flapping while I had been away – there was now a flap in his door upstairs, as well in my front door, so both cats were free to come and go at will. And in those lonely days, I found their presence an unexpected comfort.

Of course, I went to work, and I had the odd meal upstairs with Archie, who seemed to think I needed feeding up. I did my weekly stint in the Good Intentions Bookshop, and I walked for miles along the shore, and tried very hard not to think about Albert. I also caught up with Rita.

She had rung to invite me for an after-work drink in yet another newly opened little bistro, and I was pleased to see that it looked a good deal more promising than the previous one. I was less pleased to see that she was not alone.

'Johanna, I don't think you've met my colleague, Campbell Pearce? He's got an hour to waste before he has to catch his train to Dublin, so I invited him to join us.'

It was a set-up, of course. I knew it the moment I laid eyes on him, because he was about my age, and no lawyer has an hour to waste, unless there's the possibility of turning it to some advantage.

'Do you live in Dublin?' I enquired, as he handed me my drink.

'No, I'm based in Edinburgh, but I come to Belfast and Dublin regularly.'

His voice had a nice Scottish burr and he was certainly presentable – and attentive. I could see Rita smirking complacently as we discovered mutual interests, and I have to admit that an hour passed very pleasantly before he glanced at his watch and said, regretfully, that he would have to go.

'But I hope we can do this again sometime. I'll be back in Belfast in a fortnight. It's been a great pleasure to meet you, Johanna.'

'Well?' said Rita, the moment he was out of earshot. 'What do you think?'

'Very nice. For you or for me?'

'Don't be silly, he's far too old and civilised for me.'

'True. But what makes you think he's right for me?'

'You've got a lot in common,' said Rita. 'You're roughly the same age, you're both single, and you like music and travel. What's not to like?'

'He's not Albert.'

'Too right he's not. From what you've told me, he's got a lot more hair, for one thing. And at least Campbell has actually divorced his wife.'

I sighed. 'I'm sorry, Rita. He seemed a really nice man, but he's just not my type.'

'And what exactly is your type, Johanna?' Rita snapped her fingers for the waiter. 'So far you have shown a predilection for tall, dark and handsome criminals, and tall, bald and dithering academics. Apart from their height and nationality, the only thing they seem to have in common is their unreliability.'

There was a temporary lull while Rita instructed the waiter to bring us another carafe and a plate of meze, but that done, she returned to the attack.

'Look, Johanna, I know you're still yearning for your useless Albert, but it's time you moved on. And here's a lovely, sensible, successful Scot who's obviously taken with you – why can't you give him a chance?'

I shook my head. 'It's too soon.'

'Rubbish,' said Rita. 'It's never too soon. Oh well, Campbell will be snapped up by someone else, and you'll end up resorting to internet dating.'

'What's wrong with internet dating?' I looked at her in surprise. 'Doesn't everyone do it? I thought it was considered perfectly respectable these days.'

'They do and it is,' said Rita. 'But they all tell lies about themselves. They put up photos taken twenty years ago and then turn up with hearing aids and paunches and want to talk about their divorces. You'll see.'

'No I won't,' I replied, 'because it is not something I am ever going to do. Anyway, how did you meet …?' I struggled to remember the name of her current toy boy.

'Vladimir? I spotted him in a wine bar and was immediately attracted. So I went straight up to him and said, Excuse me, you're not Algernon Woodcroft, by any chance?'

'Why Algernon Woodcroft?'

'I thought the answer was unlikely to be yes.'

'And then?'

'He said he wasn't and I said, what a pity, I was hoping it would be you, but I'm so late he's probably left by now. To which he replied, why don't I buy you a drink instead? *Voilà!*'

I gazed at her with unbounded admiration. 'I could never do that! You're so … focused!'

Which just went to show why Rita was a top-flight lawyer with an endless supply of adoring men in tow, while I was an impoverished part-time seller of dodgy antiques and second-hand books, with only the prospect of seedy internet Romeos to comfort me in my declining years.

Chapter 16

It wasn't long before I was starting to regret my refusal to consider getting to know Campbell. The weekends in particular were a desert of emptiness. I took myself to the cinema, went for long walks, and eked out cups of coffee in cafes where everyone else seemed happily attached to friends or family. And one Sunday, with nothing better to do, and no particular aim in sight, I drove myself up over the hills and down to Dundonald. Turning east, a colourful mural of a dolmen caught my eye, and I suddenly remembered that there was one somewhere close at hand that Albert and I had always meant to visit.

The Traveller's Guide to Ancient County Down was still tucked away in the glove compartment, so I followed the directions of M. Heaney and found the Kempe Stones without much difficulty. They are basalt, and when excavated in the nineteenth century, were found to contain human bones. Rooks were cawing in a stand of high trees, the sun was shining fitfully on the surrounding fields, and it was a perfectly respectable dolmen – but I felt no pleasure at all. Somehow all the joy of the hunt had gone: without Albert, I felt empty.

So I turned my back on the Kempe Stones and drove towards Bangor, then on through the little coastal villages of Groomsport and Donaghadee. According to M. Heaney, there was a holy well in the grounds of one of the churches at Donaghadee, but I didn't have the heart to look for it. Instead I spent some time sitting on a bench and gazing bleakly out to sea, before I turned back inland and drove home in the late afternoon through Greyabbey. But as I retraced the route that I had so often driven with Albert, along the shore of Strangford Lough, I was suddenly so overcome with grief that I had to stop the car. Drawing off the road into a deserted lay-by, I buried my head in my arms and wept.

I cried until my sleeves were soaked, but in the end I straightened up and looked at myself in the mirror. 'Johanna,' I said, 'this will not do. Grandmother van Heerden would be ashamed of you, not to mention Great-Granny Daubenton who was famous for defending her farmstead against a whole battalion of soldiers. You must pull yourself together.'

Frederika had been right, I thought: the best possible cure for my misery would be to throw myself heart and soul into some new project. The question was, though, what should it be? And at that precise moment the sun broke through the clouds. It illuminated the far side of the lough, and the distant

Mournes, and all the little hills and hummocks of County Down, and the answer came to me as clearly as if Grandmother van Heerden had spoken the words herself: 'Don't let your present unhappiness sour the memories of your journeys. Turn them to good account, Johanna: celebrate them – write them down!'

And that is when I decided to write my own book: part travelogue, part memoir and part guide to my adopted country. I would begin with County Down and when that was done I would explore the other five counties, one by one. It was exactly the sort of long-term project that I needed, and I didn't need anyone's help: I would do it on my own.

Of course the story of my love for Albert was painfully entangled with the account of my early travels, but the work involved in mapping out and recalling all our journeys proved to be wonderfully cathartic. I couldn't yet bring myself to revisit the places we had so happily discovered together, but I have a good memory, and I had my notebooks, not to mention M. Heaney's guide to help me. Once committed to the task, I became so driven that I thought of little else. And on the days that I worked in Archibald's Antiques, I threw myself into such a frenzy of dusting, tidying and reorganising that Archie eventually begged me to stop.

'Johanna, if you go on like this, no one will recognise the place! Can't you go back to reading? Or take up some inoffensive hobby – embroidery perhaps?'

'I'm sorry, Archie. I know I'm a bit frantic at the moment. Perhaps I'll pop down to Good Intentions and buy myself a couple of good books.'

So with Archie's blessing I took myself off down the street and was pleased to find Sybilla in the bookshop.

'Sybilla,' I said, 'for reasons too painful to go into, I need something totally absorbing to read. Have you any suggestions?'

'Crime,' said Sybilla instantly, and I remembered that she was addicted to the genre. Dolores had once suggested that Sybilla must be reading all those thrillers with a view to working out how to murder her loathsome husband Roger, but sadly that was not the case. 'A good bit of noir is what you need,' she continued. 'Here, try this … and this … and this.' She picked out half a dozen books, charged me the princely sum of five pounds and thanked me for my enquiries after Percy the parrot, whose health had recently been troublesome. 'And don't forget that we can always use a bit more of your help in here if you have any time on your hands, Johanna – especially on a Saturday.'

I suspected from this last remark that she already knew about my broken romance, although up until then only Archie and Sticky Wicket had been told the reasons for Albert's absence from my life. But that is one of the hazards of living in such a small and interconnected community: secrets are very hard to keep, everyone knows everyone's business, and it is hard to go anywhere without bumping into someone you know – often the person you least expect to see.

The truth of this observation was confirmed when I came out of Mulligan's – I had noticed a special offer on my way back to Archie's: three bottles of acceptable Chenin Blanc for ten pounds – and found myself face to face with my ex-husband.

'Socrates,' I said, without enthusiasm. 'What are you doing in Belfast?'

'Oh, just a bit of business,' he responded mysteriously, while craning his neck to see what was clinking in my carrier bag. 'I'm sorry to hear about your trouble, by the way – Ellie was telling me that you'd parted company with that Albert fella. Can't say I took to him myself, but I'm sorry to hear he's let you down. It must have been a shock.'

Almost as much of a shock as the first time *you* disappeared without a word for several weeks, I might have said, but the same thought had probably occurred to him, because he hurried on: 'If there's anything I can do to help, you know you have only to say the word.'

'Good heavens, Socrates, I can't imagine why I didn't think of calling on you at once! Now I wonder what you could think of that might possibly help?'

'Well, I could go round and give the bastard a good kicking,' he suggested.

I closed my eyes briefly while several rejoinders chased themselves through my head, but in the end I didn't bother.

I just stepped round him, clinking, and continued on my way.

A week later I happened to find myself working in the Good Intentions bookshop with one of the volunteers whom I hadn't seen for several months: an attractive, energetic, but terminally interfering young woman called Susan.

'Johanna!' said Susan, clasping both my hands tightly in hers the moment she saw me. 'My dear, how *are* you?'

There is something remarkably irritating about being addressed as 'my dear' by a woman who is a lot younger than you are, but as her intentions were probably kind, I did my best to smile.

'I'm very well, thank you, Susan. And how are you?'

'Oh, my dear, I can see that you're putting a brave face on things, and I do so admire you for your courage! But you don't have to pretend with me – I know that you must be going through a truly dreadful time.'

The shop was empty, apart from Professor Humphrey, who was completely uninterested in anything other than the more obscure branches of Ecclesiology, besides being as deaf as a post. Susan, however, continued to speak in the hushed tones more usually reserved for addressing the recently bereaved.

'The breakdown of any relationship is such a dreadful blow, at any age, and you must be absolutely devastated! I just want you to know that there are those who care about you more than you might realise …'

I disengaged my hands. 'Thank you, Susan. I am grateful for your concern, but I am curious to know how you came to be so well informed?'

'It was your ex-husband Socrates, actually, who told me what had happened.'

She was beginning to look slightly uncomfortable, but as I didn't trust myself to speak, I simply raised an eyebrow and waited for her to continue.

'He came into the shop some time ago and introduced himself,' Susan explained. 'Now, I know you have had your differences, Johanna, and of course there are always two sides to every story, but if you could have seen how *deeply* concerned he was about you …'

'Really? You amaze me.'

'Johanna, please don't take offence. I hope I recognise genuine concern and sincerity when I see them, and your recent unhappiness has tortured him. He feels things so deeply – that Greek sense of family …'

'Socrates hasn't got a drop of Greek blood in his body,' I interrupted. 'He was named after a footballer.'

Susan looked briefly taken aback, but ploughed on all the same. 'Well, be that as it may, it was very plain to me that he still loves and worries about you. Of course, we all have our different ways of coping, but at times like these it's so easy to let oneself get … erm … run down.'

'Susan, what exactly did Socrates say?'

She wrung her hands, while I fought the inclination to wring her neck.

'Well, he mentioned that you might be drinking rather more than usual. It just slipped out, Johanna, that he'd run into you in the middle of the day with a bag full of bottles and you were looking very dazed and unwell. Perfectly understandable in the circumstances, of course, but he just wanted to make sure that your friends were keeping an eye on you, with all your children being so far away, and he himself so busy setting up in business again …'

'And I don't suppose he suggested that you might like to make a little investment in one of these businesses?'

'Certainly not! Well, not yet, anyway … but I can't help admiring him for having the courage to start all over again after losing everything in Africa. But that's neither here nor there, the main thing is that he's worried about your health, and I just feel I'd be failing you as a friend if I didn't do what I could to help.'

I can hardly blame other women for falling for Socrates's charm – I did so myself – but I'd heard enough.

'Well, Susan,' I said, 'I hope you will believe me when I tell you that you have nothing to concern yourself with other than your extreme gullibility and your unfortunate tendency to interfere in other people's business. But if you do still want someone to worry about, you can worry about Socrates, because the next time I see him, I'm going to kill him.'

It was probably a good thing that Professor Humphrey chose that moment to dislodge a whole row of weighty tomes which crashed to the floor, narrowly missing his ancient head, and giving me a good excuse to go to his aid. By the time order had been restored, the shop had filled up with customers and Susan and I were able to avoid any further reference to personal matters.

As luck would have it, however, I was alone that evening, sitting at my computer with a blameless cup of cocoa, when my doorbell rang. For a moment my heart stood still – I had just been writing about one of my journeys with Albert and my immediate thought was that it might be him. When I opened the front door, however, it wasn't Albert who stood on the top step, but Socrates.

'Johanna!' He beamed at me and flung open his arms expansively. Socrates has put on a bit of weight over the years, and his hair has silvered, which is a shame because it makes him look more trustworthy.

'I was hoping you might be in. I was just on my way back to Dublin when I thought, why not stay up in Belfast one more night? Give me a chance to nip down and look in on Johanna – so here I am.'

'And were you thinking of staying here?' I enquired.

'Well now, that's not a bad idea. It's been a long time since we had a chance to catch up properly.'

'That's true,' I said. 'Probably not since the time we all had to go into hiding for six weeks.'

'Oh well, if that's the way you choose to see things, there's not much that I can say.' Socrates gave a sorrowful shrug – the very picture of a man accustomed to cruel and unjust accusations. 'I just wish for your own sake that you could learn to put the past behind you, Johanna. You only hurt yourself when you bear grudges – but I won't go on, I can see you're at a bit of a low ebb right now. That's why I called round, actually: I thought you could probably do with a bit of company.'

'How very kind of you,' I replied. 'Your concern is overwhelming. In fact, I understand from Susan that you are particularly worried about my drinking.'

He had the grace to look slightly disconcerted. 'Ah now, Johanna, of course not, she must have misunderstood me … I was only in there having a bit of a chat about things in general. I've been thinking of getting involved in the charity business myself, you know.'

'Have you really?' His expression of earnest good intention would have done credit to a vicar. 'Well, at least it explains your sudden interest in rekindling our relationship. What were you planning? To use the Good Intentions model as a front for one of your dodgy enterprises?'

Socrates looked hurt. 'Ah now, Johanna, there's no call for that. I may have had to cut a few corners in my time, and I'm the first to admit I've made the odd error of judgement, but that's the nature of business – you have to be prepared to take some risks.' He gave another shrug. 'We all make mistakes when we're young – the thing to do is to face up to them like a man, then put it all behind you, and move on. And be honest, Johanna, even you would have to admit that we had a lot of fun along the way.'

Unfortunately this was also true, and he must have seen a momentary softening in my expression, because he made the mistake of stepping closer.

'Come on, darling, why don't we just bury the hatchet and let bygones be bygones? If I can do it, so can you!' He gave his old disarming smile. 'After all, we're none of us getting any younger, sweetheart, and I don't mind telling you that every time I see you, I think what a fine-looking woman you are. That old flame still burns, you know.'

'Well, let's see if this will put it out,' I said. And bending down, I picked up the jug of water I had meant to empty into the birdbath earlier, and which was still waiting just inside the door – and I emptied it over Socrates instead. Then I slammed the door shut in his face.

It was reprehensible, I know, and childish. But it was deeply satisfying.

Chapter 17

Time trundled on. I stopped waiting for the phone to ring
– indeed, the few times it did ring, it was usually one of the
children making tactful enquiries about my state of mind,
Socrates having told anyone who would listen that I was
showing alarming signs of going off my head. I also made plans
to visit Finn and Marta for Christmas, and I worked away at my
book. By the time November came round I had achieved some
sort of equilibrium. And that, of course, is when I bumped into
Albert again.

I was walking up from the city centre, head down against the
sleety wind and muffled to the eyeballs, when I cannoned into
someone coming round a corner and found myself looking up
into the face that I knew and loved so well.

'Albert!'

'Johanna!'

'Albert!'

This might have gone on for some time if someone else

hadn't shouldered me out of the way. Albert grasped my arm to steady me and the familiar shock ran through me. I would swear it ran through him too because his grip tightened and I thought for one glorious moment that he was going to pull me into his arms. Instead he cleared his throat and said, 'You're looking well, Johanna.'

'No I'm not, and neither are you.'

'Well, the last few months have been very hard on me.'

'For me too, Albert – for me too.' Suddenly I was overcome with fury. 'Why haven't you phoned or emailed?'

'The last time I rang, you put the phone down on me,' said Albert. 'And then Sidney said you were in London.'

Sidney? Sidney? I thought wildly, until I realised he was talking about Sticky Wicket.

'I ran into him in B&Q,' said Albert.

I'd forgotten their mutual interest in DIY Really, it was amazing how well the men in my life got on with each other – he'd be going to antiques fairs with Archie next.

'And then I ran into your ex-husband Socrates,' Albert continued. 'He was surprisingly friendly – he told me that you were back together again.' How like Socrates, I thought, to do his best to ensure that if he didn't get what he wanted, then neither would anybody else. 'So there didn't seem any point in trying to get in touch …'

'Oh Albert, what a fool you are!' I said sadly, but I got no further because at that moment there was a call of 'Daddy!

We're over here.' And looking across the road, I saw three women. Norah and Rosie I recognised at once; the third, who was swathed in a dark green cloak, could only have been Carmel. Even from a distance I could see her likeness to Norah and – honesty unfortunately impels me to admit – her beauty, but any possible doubt as to her identity was removed by the hunted expression that had instantly appeared on Albert's face.

'I'm sorry,' he said, 'but I'll have to go. It's wedding business: we're meeting Kevin's parents for lunch ...'

'Don't worry,' I replied. 'I wouldn't dream of detaining you a moment longer. Goodbye, Albert.' And blinded by sleet and tears I pushed past him and blundered on up the street.

Archie took one look at me when I came through the door and hurried off to make a mug of coffee, into which he poured a slug of brandy. As I sobbed out the story of my encounter, he murmured sympathetically; then he very sweetly insisted on driving me home.

'I'm so sorry it's my bridge club party tonight,' he said. 'I'd have taken you out to dinner otherwise. Tomorrow, perhaps?'

I patted his hand. 'What a kind man you are, Archie. But I'm feeling better already, I promise – it must be the brandy. And I've got any number of things planned to do this weekend, so don't you worry about me.'

In truth, I had nothing planned for the weekend, and very little to look forward to in the run-up to Christmas, apart from the annual Good Intentions party. Dolores had screeched to a halt outside Archibald's Antiques that very morning, and lowered the window to issue her invitation.

'Christmas party for all the volunteers: first Sunday in December, my house at seven o'clock. Make sure you come! Yes, I know it's a bus stop' – this to a red-coated traffic warden who had suddenly appeared – 'but this is a vital message I'm passing on, and there isn't a bus in sight. Anyway, why aren't you doing something about that van that's blocking the traffic down the road, instead of picking on pensioners?'

She zoomed off as he turned to look for the offending van, and by the time he had concluded that it was no longer there – or, indeed, had quite possibly never been there in the first place – Dolores had disappeared around the corner.

We looked at each other and shrugged. Then he sighed rather theatrically before continuing on his thankless round, while I let myself into the shop to make a note of the party in my otherwise sadly empty diary.

My diary might have been empty but at least there were several emails waiting for me when I got home, including one from Frederika, and one from Seamus, who apologised for not being in touch but wanted to know if it was okay if he didn't pay me the last £50 he owed me until after Christmas. Seamus, in true student fashion, was always paying off debts in instalments to those of his relatives foolish enough to lend him any money in the first place. I dealt with his email first.

✉ From: johannavanheerden@hotmail.com
   To: seamusvanshea@gmail.com

   Dear Seamus,
   Please don't worry about your several
   weeks' silence – or the money. It is
   true that I am a lonely, neglected and
   impoverished old pensioner but I don't
   eat much, and Sticky Wicket is unlikely
   to evict me if I don't pay the rent,
   so I can probably struggle on until
   January. And if all else fails I
   can eat Tiger Lily.
   Love from your mother.

Then I turned to Freddy, who was in her usual good form.

✉ From: cosmictraveller@yahoo.co.za
   To: johannavanheerden@hotmail.com

   Hello darling,
   Just back from Zanzibar. Stayed in the
   most glorious place – white sands, azure
   water. Paradise! So restoring.

Next time I'm going to take you with
me. How are you doing? And when are you
coming home? Thandi says to tell you that
the New Year is looking particularly
auspicious for travel.
I miss you!
F xxxx

✉ From: johannavanheerden@hotmail.com
To: cosmictraveller@yahoo.co.za

Dear Freddy,
I'm not sure I have total confidence in
Thandi's forecasts: the last auspicious
date she gave me, there was an airline
strike. Still, I'm glad you had such a
good trip. The pictures are gorgeous and
I am very jealous. The weather here is
freezing and the only entertainment I
have to look forward to at the moment
is the Good Intentions Christmas party.
Last year Basil passed out under the
table because he had forgotten to take
his tablets, and Agnes, who is normally
the soul of tact and sobriety, had a bit
too much killer punch and told Sybilla's
husband Roger that he was a wart on the
nose of humanity. (True.) I can only hope
for similar excitement this year.

I'm sorry I haven't booked my trip
home yet. I miss you terribly too but
my life has been so upside-down lately
that I just don't feel up to making any
decisions. But I'll be in London for
Christmas with all the children – Nuala
and Seamus are going to be there too – so
I'm looking forward to that.
All in all, though, I'll be glad when
this year is over.
Love
Johanna xxx

✉ From: cosmictraveller@yahoo.co.za
To: johannavanheerden@hotmail.com

Christmas is still some way off. I
hate to think of you so sad and lonely.
Have you considered internet dating?
That's how and Robert and Yoweri met.
Just a thought.
F x

✉ From: johannavanheerden@hotmail.com
To: cosmictraveller@yahoo.co.za

Rita had the same thought, but she
wasn't very encouraging. Anyway, it's
not for me.
And don't worry, I'll be fine. Off to bed

now with Tiger Lily and my book.
Love,
Johanna

But I wasn't fine. I passed a restless night, due possibly to nightmares brought on by Sybilla's choice of crime fiction, and when I woke, the rain was teeming down and I'd run out of coffee. The day went on from there: I shopped for food and found I'd left my purse at home; I forced myself to go for a walk along the shore and tripped over an uneven patch of pathway, ripping my trousers and cutting my knee. Not one of the friends I would normally have cajoled into accompanying me to the cinema or a pub was free – Rita was away on business and even Sticky Wicket was out – and I simply didn't have the heart to work on the story of my travels. By the time I had finished my solitary dinner in front of the television, I felt that things could hardly get worse – and so, in desperation, I switched on my computer, and did what I had vowed I would not do …

✉ From: johannavanheerden@hotmail.com
To: cosmictraveller@yahoo.co.za;
rita.can@aol.co.uk

Freddy and Rita, if either of you ever breathes a word of this to anyone I will never speak to you again, but I was feeling so lonely and unloved this weekend that I went online to a dating

site. And the upshot is that I am meeting
a man called Bill for a coffee on
Wednesday afternoon. He looks perfectly
normal, he's a bit younger than me, and
he likes country walks and music. If he
turns out to be an axe-murderer it will
be your fault for mentioning the subject
in the first place.
Johanna

✉ From rita.can@aol.co.uk
To: johannavanheerden@hotmail.com

Go for it, girl! Even if he is an axe-
murderer, he's unlikely to chop you up in
a coffee shop xx

✉ From: cosmictraveller@yahoo.co.za
To: johannavanheerden@hotmail.com

Harness the power of the cosmos, darling!
Have faith in yourself and believe in
your right to happiness! Just ring me
on Wednesday evening so I know you are
safely home.
Freddy xox

✉ From: johannavanheerden@hotmail.com
To: rita.can@aol.co.uk;
cosmictraveller@yahoo.co.za

How right you were, Rita – he wasn't an axe-murderer but he was *at least* ten years older than me, he wore an anorak and a bobble hat, and he wanted to talk about his divorce. I have another date on Friday with someone who is a retired accountant. I expect very little.
Johanna

✉ From: johannavanheerden@hotmail.com
To: rita.can@aol.co.uk;
cosmictraveller@yahoo.co.za

My expectations were fulfilled. We went to The Fox and Fiddle, he put his hand on my knee after the first glass of wine, and apart from asking my name and what I wanted to drink, he did not ask me a *single* other question about myself. I don't think I'm cut out for this.
Johanna

✉ From: rita.can@aol.co.uk
To: johannavanheerden@hotmail.com

Obviously not. You should have snapped up Campbell Pearce while you had the chance. Never mind, at least you'll be in London over Christmas and as soon as I get back from Paris we'll go out on the town.
Mwah xx

✉ From: cosmictraveller@yahoo.co.za
  To: johannavanheerden@hotmail.com

There is someone out there for you,
darling, I feel it in my bones. You
mustn't be so easily discouraged. Just
remember that those who see clearly with
the eyes of love, will love what they
see.
Have faith!
Freddy xxxx

✉ From: johannavanheerden@hotmail.com
  To: cosmictraveller@yahoo.co.za

All right, Freddy, I'm going to give
it one last try. I have to say there's
not much left to choose from in my age
group, but I'm going to take a chance
on 'Galahad', a retired but active
gentleman, who has a good sense of humour
and his own hair and teeth...

✉ From: johannavanheerden@hotmail.com
  To: cosmictraveller@yahoo.co.za

Oh God, Freddy, it was Sticky Wicket...

Chapter 18

Fortunately for both Sticky Wicket and me, he didn't see me. He was sitting in a corner of the cafe where we had arranged to meet, reading a copy of the *Belfast Telegraph* and a sporting a flower in his buttonhole, as agreed. I backed out as swiftly and surreptitiously as I could, then fled home to compose a message from 'Magdalena D' to the effect that she greatly regretted having had to let him down but urgent family business had required her to leave the country at short notice.

I was particularly kind to Sticky Wicket for the next few days, which was probably why he offered me a lift to Dolores's house the following Sunday.

I had been planning to ring for a cab but Sticky wouldn't hear of it. 'No trouble at all,' he boomed, when I told him of my plans. 'Be a pleasure. Got a bit of a do at the golf club on Sunday, as it happens, and I can just as easily go that way. Pick you up afterwards too, if you like.'

'That's very kind, but I've no idea when I'll want to leave and anyway I'm sure to get a lift. If not, I can take a cab.'

We were standing in the front hall during this exchange, sorting through a heap of mail that the postman had just delivered. Sticky handed me an envelope addressed to J.M. van Heerden.

'Often meant to ask you what the "M" stands for,' he said.

'Maria,' I answered, which wasn't true, I am afraid, but if I'd told him Magdalena the penny would undoubtedly have dropped.

So on Sunday evening, Sticky Wicket dropped me off and I climbed the three steps to Dolores's front door with a mild sense of anticipation. There was a holly wreath above the brass knocker, the door was ajar, a Christmas tree stood in the hallway, and Dolores herself was taking coats from a man and woman I hadn't met before.

'Johanna! You look wonderful!' She embraced me warmly. 'I don't think you know Iris and Max? Come along in …'

She propelled us through double doors and into one of those lovely, traditional rooms that feel so welcoming and festive on a winter's night. An abundance of Christmas cards and decorations surrounded a real log fire, and from a burnished tureen on a table just inside the door, Charles was ladling out mulled wine.

Charles and Dolores have an odd but happy relationship: he spends the summers in his house in Italy, and the rest of the year with Dolores in Belfast. Sybilla says that six months with Dolores is as much as anyone could stand but Dolores herself maintains that she doesn't like 'Abroad', and having been married twice, she knows that the secret to a happy relationship is long periods spent apart.

'Hello, Charles,' I said, accepting his kiss and a glass of mulled wine. 'What a dashing waistcoat!'

'Hand-painted by Dolores several years ago. Fortunately it was a short-lived hobby.' He winked. 'I only wear it on very special occasions.'

It was certainly an eye-catching garment, with a vivid pattern of green and yellow splodges on a scarlet background, but it was no more startling than some of the other outfits on display. The Good Intentions volunteers are a disparate and eccentric lot, and their party clothes reflected this: Dylan, resplendent in an Irish kilt, was chatting to Agnes, who was in floor-length mauve lace, while a pale girl called Phoebe, who was wearing what looked like a Victorian nightdress with clumpy boots and a little knitted hat, clung to the arm of a boy in jeans and a leather jacket. I could see why my own unremarkable clothing had impressed Dolores.

There were always a few people at these affairs whom I hadn't met before – partners, or new recruits, or volunteers whose shifts had never coincided with mine – but most of them I knew reasonably well. As I ran my eye over the crowd, I saw with relief that Susan appeared to be absent. Nor was there any sign of Sybilla's husband.

'Poor Roger – he had a migraine coming on,' she explained. 'I'm not surprised, though – I thought yesterday that he was looking very out of sorts.'

I only just stopped myself from asking 'How on earth could you tell?' – Roger being a permanently sour-looking individual whose appeal to Sybilla was unfathomable.

Of course, we all knew perfectly well that it was the previous year's confrontation with Agnes that had kept him away. The reason for Susan's absence from the party, however, was more surprising, as I discovered when Dolores took me aside and asked if I'd heard the news.

'No. What's happened?'

'Well, Susan told me she couldn't be here this evening because she had to drive down to Clogher unexpectedly, to spend the weekend with an ailing aunt. But on Friday night she was spotted at the airport – waiting to board a plane, with a man who wasn't her husband!'

'Perhaps it was her cousin or her brother and they had decided to fly down to visit the aunt?'

'Don't be silly, Johanna. You can't fly to Clogher: I'd be surprised if they've got a bus stop there, never mind an airport. Anyway, they were holding hands, and you don't hold hands with your cousin – and certainly not your brother – not in Northern Ireland.'

'I don't suppose he was tall, silver-haired and handsome?'

'Why? Do you know who he is?'

'Well, it just so happens that Susan took it upon herself to intervene in my personal affairs recently, and it seemed to me that she might have fallen for the charms of my ex-husband Socrates …'

'Oh, I've met him,' Dolores interrupted. 'He's come slithering round the shop a couple of times, enquiring after your health and intimating that you were drinking too much. I sent him packing.'

'Good for you. A pity Susan didn't have as much sense.' And I regaled Dolores with the story of my conversation with Susan and the subsequent dousing of Socrates.

She shrieked with mirth. 'I'll have to ask Paula for a fuller description – she's the one who spotted Susan. I don't think you've met her but she's one of Kathleen's granddaughters. She works at the airport, but she sometimes helps out in the bookshop at weekends.'

It was hard to think of two people less suited to each other than Socrates and Susan, a thought that gave me some pleasure, I'm sorry to say. Mind you, I did feel a passing sympathy for anyone trying to have an illicit affair in a society where everyone kept such a close eye on each other – whatever it was that you were up to, someone, somewhere, would see you and take note.

'Well, I'd be delighted if it was Socrates Susan was with,' I said. 'It would serve them both right!'

'I've often meant to ask you, how did you meet him in the first place?' asked Dolores.

'I was on a backpacking holiday in London, and he was a student working in some pub or other. I met him in Hyde Park. I was bowled over by his Irish accent and his charm – and literally bowled over by his dog. It was a whirlwind romance.'

'What sort of dog was it?'

'I've no idea – something huge and enthusiastic. And it wasn't his dog. He'd pinched it from where it was tied up while its owner had nipped into the cafe – thought it would be a useful means of introduction.'

Dolores gave another snort of laughter, and then reached out an arm to grab the man I'd been introduced to when I first arrived. 'Here, talk to Max – I'm sure you'll have a lot in common – while I go and tell Sybilla about Susan!'

She sailed off, leaving me with Max, a slight, gentle man with beautiful manners, who had arrived with Iris but was single. On the face of it, this was all we had in common, discreet questioning having swiftly elicited the information that Max was a recently-retired civil servant who had never been to Africa, was almost certainly gay, and didn't particularly like cats. However, he was a keen bridge player and inevitably, he knew Archie.

'I see him at the club quite regularly. He sings your praises.'

'Thank you. Well, I love Archie and it's a pleasure to work for him.'

'And such an intriguing little shop, I always think.'

'Indeed. He's a rather intriguing character himself. Full of surprises.'

'I suppose you mean those rather dreadful books he writes?'

'You know about them?'

'Oh, we all know about them, we just don't mention the subject because we know he'd be utterly mortified.'

If I had needed any further proof that evening that absolutely nothing in this part of the world could be kept a secret, it was provided at supper. Agnes and I had taken seats next to Kathleen at a small table in one corner of the room. Kathleen is a great favourite of mine. She is unfailingly kind and interested in those around her, and a tremendous talker who rarely finishes a sentence – which grasshopper-like quality in her conversation I attribute to her having had an enormous family and a lifetime spent doing a thousand things at once. At any rate, we were all three happily addressing our turkey and ham when Agnes suddenly froze.

'Don't look round now!' she hissed. 'It's Mary …'

With one accord we bent over our plates, but it was too late – Mary, a famously lugubrious and dedicated hypochondriac, had loomed up behind us like a cold front and there was nothing for it but to shift up and make room.

'Thank you, dear.' She settled herself beside me. 'I thought I was never going to find a seat. My poor old back is playing up again – I wouldn't be at all surprised if there's more bad weather on the way.' She gave a deep sigh, then poked doubtfully at the food on her plate. 'I do hope there isn't anything too spicy in this. I had terrible indigestion the last time.'

'It's delicious,' said Agnes, 'and not at all spicy.'

'Isn't Dolores so good, doing this every year?' Kathleen shook her head in amazement. 'Always such a wonderful spread, I wonder does she go to Orr's ...'

'I couldn't come last year,' Mary interrupted. 'It was just after Harold's accident, and I wasn't well myself of course. Not at all. I wasn't a bit surprised when I found I had shingles.'

'Oh dear, that's so painful!' Kathleen patted her hand. 'I had it once ...'

'I've had it three times so far.' Mary spoke with grim pride, and Agnes, who was on my other side, rose abruptly to her feet. 'It'll be her diverticulitis next,' she muttered to me. 'I'm off to get another drink.'

She left us to our fate, while I made a feeble stab at directing the conversation along more cheerful lines.

'Well,' I said, 'it's lovely to see you looking so well now, Mary. And you've got a new hairstyle.'

This temporarily distracted her. 'I had it done for a wedding yesterday.' She patted the iron waves complacently. 'It was a beautiful wedding. Such a lovely young couple: Kevin – he's my cousin's son, the cousin that died from septicaemia – and Norah, she's ...' She stopped short. 'But I think you might know her, Johanna: Norah Morrow. I'm sure I saw you with her father once. I was coming out the surgery and you were getting into his car.'

Fortunately, Dolores chose that moment to announce the arrival of dessert, and I seized the opportunity to make my escape.

'Can I bring either of you some Christmas pudding?' I asked. 'And it looks as though Charles is breaking out the champagne.'

'Champagne! What a treat.' Kathleen clapped her hands in delight, which made me feel more than a little guilty about abandoning her as well, but on these occasions it's every woman for herself. As I made for safety I heard Mary say, 'Champagne? Oh no, I don't think so, dear, just a small mince pie for me. But you go ahead and enjoy yourself, while you still can.'

I spent the next hour or so doing my best to enjoy myself, and succeeded rather well. By eleven o'clock we had all been well fed, and possibly too well watered, because a heated argument broke out suddenly between Dylan and one of the other volunteers. I'm not sure anyone knew what it was about, but I sidled up to Dolores and suggested that it might be time we all went home.

'Shall I start the ball rolling and ring for a cab?'

It was Kathleen who gave me a lift home, however – or rather, her husband John did. He was one of those large, slow, silent men, but there was a twinkle in his eye, and he and Kathleen had been married for fifty years. As I waved them goodbye and let myself into my flat, I reflected sadly on the fact that so few people I knew had long-lasting and companionable relationships – or even unaccountable ones like Sybilla and Roger's. But apart from that, and the pang I had felt at the mention of Kevin and Norah's wedding, it had been an unexpectedly happy evening.

Sticky Wicket had not returned, but Tiger Lily was curled up in the middle of my bed. She opened one eye disapprovingly when I gave a gentle hiccup.

I pretended not to notice. 'Do you know,' I told her, 'I feel better than I have done for a very long time. I think I might be on the mend at last!' And for the first time in weeks, I fell asleep at once and slept like a log until morning.

Chapter 19

Disappointingly, it turned out that Susan's mystery man wasn't Socrates at all, but rather a dance instructor called Harry. Still, as Dolores said, when relaying this piece of information, not only did Susan have a husband of her own, the man in question was reputed to have a wife in Letterkenny, so that would give us enough ammunition to keep her in her place for the foreseeable future.

More distressing to me was the report in a local paper, a couple of days later, of the wedding of Norah Morrow to Kevin Dunne. There was a photograph of the happy couple with the bride's parents, Mr and Mrs Albert Morrow. Carmel appeared to be wearing a fur lampshade on her head, but that was small comfort: she still looked distressingly beautiful, and she had her arm linked through Albert's in a proprietorial manner. Albert himself looked mildly alarmed, but as that was his habitual expression, it wasn't much comfort either.

Fortunately I had Christmas in London to look forward to. I

did feel briefly guilty about abandoning both Sticky Wicket and Archie to their solitary celebrations, but my concerns turned out to have been misplaced – Archie assured me that he would be having a slap-up lunch with friends from the bridge club, and Sticky, when I enquired about his plans, grew unexpectedly pink.

'Been invited out, actually.'

'Oh, somewhere nice?'

'Friend's house. Don't think you know her.' His ears had begun to glow like beacons. 'Called Vera.'

I was tempted to ask him how he had met her – and, indeed, whether she had her own hair and teeth – but he was so covered in confusion that I decided not to tease him. Instead I kissed him on his blushing cheek, wished him a very happy Christmas, and went back downstairs to finish my packing.

I arrived in London to find the Organic Ashram full to bursting – Ellie was still living with Finn and Marta, Nuala and Seamus had arrived the day before, and Sophie (famous for her turnip and lentil stew) had been replaced by a charming pair of Swedish ballet dancers, much to Pippa's delight. So charmed was she, indeed, that she followed them around constantly – dressed in a grubby pink tutu and leg warmers – and did her best to emulate their languid grace. There was also a new addition to the house in the shape of a rescue dog called Pocket, who in turn followed Pippa everywhere, bringing up the rear of a small comic procession that moved about the house, with the twins and their cameras filming them as they went.

It simply wasn't possible to be unhappy in the middle of such a lively crowd, and Christmas went by in a blur of food, drink, presents and laughter. But I didn't stay on for New Year because Socrates was planning to join the party and it was only fair to let the children have some time with him alone. Also, given the circumstances of our last encounter, and my murderous feelings towards him since I had spoken to Albert, I felt it was probably wiser to avoid a meeting.

So, with a promise to return as soon as the new baby was born – and with another to Pippa that she could come over to Belfast for a visit on her own, or with Ellie, in the Easter holidays – I flew back to see in the New Year with Tiger Lily.

I had received several invitations to spend New Year's Eve with friends – even Sticky Wicket had manfully suggested that I might like to join a party at the golf club – but I had declined them all. I was determined to stay quietly at home and see the old year out with the stoicism that I hoped would carry me through the dark and lonely months to come. Besides, I was in no mood for company and I had a very real fear that one drink would lead to several more, and eventually to maudlin self-pity. I did in fact have a bottle of champagne in the fridge, sent by

Rita who was sunning herself with friends in the Caribbean, but I planned to keep it for a happier occasion – should one ever again arise.

Instead I sat down at my desk and prepared to write my last email of the year.

✉ From: johannavanheerden@hotmail.com
To: cosmictraveller@yahoo.co.za

Darling Freddy,
I'm glad you had such a merry Christmas. I must say my own Christmas was a lot happier than expected and the children made a huge fuss of me. They are all looking well – Ellie is back to her old self, I'm glad to say, and Marta is positively blooming.
Anyway, here I am, back home again, missing them all terribly, and wondering what you are up to. Is the Kalk Bay Moon Circle performing some ancient rite on the beach tonight, I wonder? Perhaps I should open a branch here – that would certainly give the neighbours something to talk about! I can't face going out, so I am going to have my supper and then tuck myself up with hot milk and honey, and the cats. It's not what I thought I would be doing a few months ago!

But enough of that! Tomorrow, you will
be glad to hear, I am going to begin
again. I am going to count my blessings
– my family, my friends, and thank God,
my health – and try to see this last year
as something that was wonderful while it
lasted, but was always doomed to end – a
sort of unexpected sunset cruise. The
one thing I know for certain is that I
am just too old for any more heartbreak,
so no more romance for me! My New Year's
resolution is to put this whole year
behind me and think sensibly about the
future – which might very well mean
that I'll decide to move. Will keep you
posted.
I'm going to switch off all the phones
now because I do *not* want cheerful
messages from anyone at midnight. I'll
phone you tomorrow instead.
Happy New Year and love as ever,
Johanna xxxx

I did not hear the bells and horns, or see the fireworks of New
Year, because I had earplugs in my ears and a mask over my
eyes. Also I had, for the very last time, cried myself to sleep. I
wept for the loss of Albert, for his voice in the night and his
arms around me, and for all the adventures we might still have

shared. And when I woke to a stone-grey winter day, I pulled on several layers of clothes, thrust my feet into fur-lined boots and my head into a woollen hat, and went for a long and thoughtful tramp along the shore.

There was no one else about – even the dog walkers had decided it was too early and too cold. The far side of the lough was shrouded in mist and the Cave Hill had the icy sheen of frost. Somewhere out of sight, in a jumble of red brick houses, Albert would still be sleeping. Or perhaps he was in his kitchen, drinking tea and savouring a little peace and quiet before the New Year's Day round of friends and family began. I realised now that the idea of the two of us sharing a house in loving companionship in our declining years had always been deeply unrealistic. I didn't doubt that Albert had loved me, but he was, and always would be, too tightly bound by family ties and convention, and too fearful of upheaval at this stage of his life, to make any permanent changes.

I, on the other hand, had little choice. I wasn't just getting older, I was lonely, and I no longer had any family on this island. Ellie would either stay on in London or resume her travels, and the twins were unlikely to return for more than fleeting visits. I had good friends, certainly, but they would manage very well without me – or, like Rita, who thought nothing of flying half way round the world for a weekend, would have no difficulty keeping in touch. Sticky Wicket would easily find another tenant and be happy to inherit Tiger Lily and Archie would find another assistant, or better still, embrace a life of retirement. He might even join Sticky Wicket and Albert at cricket matches where they could have the occasional nostalgic conversation about Johanna and the upheaval she had caused in all their lives – then sigh with relief that peace and normality had eventually been restored. In short, it was time to go.

I turned back towards home feeling curiously cleansed and empty now that I had come to a final decision. I would cut my losses and move to England in the spring, to be closer to Finn and Marta. I would be a doting grandmother to the new baby and to Pippa; I would visit museums and galleries and go to concerts; and I would make new friends and stay in touch with old ones. But this time when I left the north of Ireland, I would not return.

'That's the spirit,' said the voice of Granny van Heerden in my ear. 'Put it all behind you and move on!' And I sensed Great-Grandmother Daubenton nodding in agreement.

Back home I made a pot of tea, then I sat down at my computer to complete the section of my book that dealt with County Down. I doubted that the rest of it would ever be written now, but that was just too bad. I was soon absorbed in my task, and not at all pleased when half an hour later there was a tap at my door. It would be Sticky Wicket, I knew, looking for milk or aspirin.

But it wasn't Sticky Wicket who stood in the hallway – it was Albert.

'Your front door was open, Johanna.'

'Oh, I must not have closed it properly when I came back in.'

'You've been out walking?'

'Yes.'

'So have I.' There was a pause. 'I hope you don't mind but I just dropped by to give you something …'

I held the door to my flat open. 'Come in, if you like.'

He looked nervously over my shoulder. 'If you're sure it's not inconvenient?'

'If you mean, am I alone, the answer is yes. Who did you think might be inside? Sticky Wicket?'

'Well, I wasn't sure. After speaking to your ex-husband …'

'Forget Socrates. There was never the slightest chance of us getting back together. But you might at least have checked with me.'

'Yes.'

We stepped inside.

'And you and Carmel? Any chance of a reconciliation there?'

'None whatever, I'm glad to say.' Another silence. 'I've put the house back on the market, by the way.'

'Oh good. We'll both be moving then.'

'You're moving house?'

'Yes. I'm going to England to be closer to my children. As you can imagine, there's not much reason to stay here now.'

Albert appeared to be trembling. It was all I could do not to put out a steadying arm as I waited for him to speak.

'The thing is, Johanna, that I feel so bad about the way things ended between us … I was hoping there might be some way I could try to make amends.'

'What did you have in mind?'

'Well, to apologise for a start. To say how sorry I am that I let you down, that my inability to manage things properly caused you so much pain.'

'Anything else?'

'That I have missed you more than I can say.'

The ghosts of grannies van Heerden and Daubenton were beginning to squawk with alarm but I closed my ears to them and held my breath. I was waiting for Albert to make the final, unequivocal, declaration of love and commitment. Instead he patted the pockets of his coat in a distracted manner and eventually extracted a small package, which he handed silently to me.

Inside the wrapping was a book – *The Traveller's Guide to Ancient County Antrim*. I opened it to find the following inscription: 'To Johanna, with all good wishes for your future travels, from the author, Marc Heaney'. Beneath that, in pencil, were the words, 'And from Albert, who was lucky enough to share your earlier travels. Love always.'

'It came out just before Christmas,' Albert said. 'I hoped you wouldn't have it yet.'

'And you got him to sign it for me?'

'I tracked him down through your friend Agnes.'

'Oh Albert!' I whispered.

'Yes, well, I'm more sorry than I can say that you've decided to move. I don't suppose there is anything I can do now that might persuade you to change your mind?'

I turned the pages of M. Heaney's book reflectively. The silence lengthened. Then I sighed.

'Well, it's probably going to take me a while to put my affairs in order – a couple of months, at least, I imagine. And in the meantime, I don't suppose one or two outings would hurt – according to M. Heaney there are a great many things in County Antrim that should not be missed.'

'Not to mention Armagh, Derry, and Fermanagh,' Albert said.

'And Tyrone,' I finished for him. 'In which case, I suppose I could be persuaded to stay on a little longer …'

I saw through the window behind him that snow had begun falling lightly. The far side of the lough had disappeared, as hidden from me as my future, which was probably a good thing, because in my experience people don't change much once they've reached a certain age, and I had no doubt at all that there would be any number of difficulties ahead. Then the view was blocked by Albert as he held out his arms and stepped towards me, and for the time being, my thoughts ceased.

Reader, life is not perfect; we rarely get exactly what we want, so we must all learn to make the most of such happiness as comes our way. After all, as my sister Frederika would say, 'It is better to travel with the Wind of Hope in your sails than to be becalmed in the Sea of Sorrow'. Or something like that.